DEDICATION

Dedicated to my parents
Nicholas and Mary Kotsonis

Eternal Memory

Two Tales
of One City

ZENOVIA KOTSONIS

ANAPHORA
PRESS

Cover photo: Saint Xenia's chapel in St. Petersburg, present day.
Sketch of Saint Xenia: Jeannette Kotsonis
Icon of Saint Xenia: Convent of St. Elizabeth the Grand Duchess,
    Etna, CA. Used by permission.
    http://www.conventofsaintelizabeth.org

Anaphora Press
3110 Port Townsend, WA 98368
anaphorapress.com

ISBN: 0980124182
ISBN-13: 978-0980124187

CONTENTS

IN THE NAME OF THE FATHER, SON
AND HOLY SPIRIT.
HERE RESTS THE BODY OF THE SERVANT-OF-GOD,
XENIA GRIGORIEVNA,
WIFE OF THE IMPERIAL CHORISTER,
COLONEL ANDREI THEODOROVICH PETROV.
WIDOWED AT THE AGE OF TWENTY-SIX,
A PILGRIM FOR FORTY-FIVE YEARS,
SHE LIVED A TOTAL OF SEVENTY-ONE YEARS.
SHE WAS KNOWN BY THE NAME
ANDREI THEODOROVICH.

MAY WHOEVER KNEW ME
PRAY FOR MY SOUL
THAT HIS OWN MAY BE SAVED.
AMEN

CHAPTER I
Leningrad, 1963

It was a rare occasion when Yelena Andreeva thought of Leningrad as being cheerful. But tonight, as she stepped off the bus at *Deskaya Street* and took a deep breath, drawing in the scent of lilacs, she could think of no better word to describe the atmosphere in the city. It was decidedly cheerful.

Hidden somewhere in a bush, a lark trilled a love song, full-throated and hopeful. The chestnut trees were in full bloom, stems stacked with white blossoms. In the chill of late May their singular earthy odor promised summer's warmth.

That time of year had arrived in the north of Russia when daytime lingers late and, like a small child who hates to leave the party, the sun refuses to go to bed. At certain special moments, in the pearlescent glow of evening daylight, the harsh Soviet gray of Leningrad's modern sections softens, taking on the lavender hue of a dove's wing.

The ride from the hospital had been long and tiring, but Yelena felt a new surge of energy now that she had nearly reached her destination. She stopped and buttoned her coat against the cold. Laying a scarf over her hair, she tied it in a secure knot under her chin, unaware of the impression she made on an elderly couple selling spring flowers from a cart on the sidewalk: a tall, slim young woman striding purposefully down the street, with four inches of blond hair (a honeyed, natural blond, not that brassy platinum so many girls were getting from a bottle in those days) visible below the point of her turquoise scarf, her green eyes bright as sea-glass as she stopped briefly to examine their wares. The man turned to his wife after Yelena had moved away, peering at her carefully. He smiled then, as if recalling, perhaps, a time when his stooped and wrinkled helpmate had presented such a picture.

The strange two-sidedness of her life struck Yelena as she continued down the street. Passing a group of men smoking on the street corner, she was as oblivious to their appreciative glances as she had been to the flower-vendor's. Yelena had spent the previous nine hours relieving pain and suffering, and fending off the depression that threatened to set in as she was forced to accept the limits of her role as healer. She had lost a twelve-year-old boy to a congenital heart condition just that morning. There was nothing she could have done; the problem was undetectable, but the grief and sorrow shown by his family had nearly overwhelmed her, making her wish that as a child she'd dreamed of becoming an engineer instead of a doctor. Here she was, enjoying the beauty of a whitening night, just a few feet away from a reunion she knew would bring her happiness. And that was difficult to reconcile with the events of the day.

The rusty iron gate leading into the *Smolensk Cemetery*

seemed to be the only thing holding together the decaying fence that surrounded it. Opening the gate carefully to avoid unhinging it, Yelena stepped through. Heeding its protesting creaks, she closed it with the same care. Densely wooded, grown over with thick, flowering vines and weeds, moldering headstones pushing up through the undergrowth like great mushrooms – the vast cemetery seemed to be lying under a spell, waiting for some storybook hero to arrive.

A few rays of light shone through a ragged opening in the forest ceiling, illuminating a small green chapel adjacent to a larger church. It was the workshop, just as Sasha had described it. Yelena's pulse raced. But as she picked her way across the grounds toward it, her heart thudded with a more solemn rhythm. Broken crosses and disintegrating monuments lay in disarray on both sides of the path.

Steeling her heart against the twinge of sorrow she felt at seeing the state of the graves, Yelena forced herself to remain unsentimental, calling to mind the fact that the crosses and graves with their religious inscriptions were relics of an embarrassing past, a past mired in a bog of ignorance and myths.

Suddenly the breeze shifted, blowing in from the *Neva River*, and a silvery blend of harmonizing voices rode it like shells washing ashore with the tide. Though it was lovely and sweetly sung, the tune was unfamiliar. Or was it? Enchanted, she drifted toward the workshop, feeling a vague bit of *déjà vu* as she knocked on the door.

"You're late," Sasha murmured into her scarf-covered ear as he hugged her close, kissing each of her cold-reddened cheeks in turn.

"I'm sorry, sweetheart, but you know how it is in my profession. Illness doesn't check the clock before it drops by unannounced. I came as quickly as I could. I've been thinking about this moment all day."

Yelena pulled away from her fiancé and held him at arms length studying his features, depositing them in her memory bank for the days of separation ahead. It was a fine face. She lifted the shock of thick hair that lay over his wide, serious forehead, revealing warm eyes, the color of graphite. His dark good looks were an inheritance from some distant Gypsy ancestor. She counted herself a lucky woman, easing back into Sasha's embrace just as he said, "What a lucky man I am."

"It's a great little workshop, Sasha. I'm so happy for you, and proud. It's about time your talents were recognized." Yelena stretched up on her toes, kissing his forehead. "Do you know it's been nearly three weeks since we've been together?"

"Seems like three years," Sasha said, drawing her close again, brushing his cheek against hers.

"How are we ever going to find an apartment, Lena? I want us to be husband and wife and I don't think I can wait much longer."

"I know, I know. I feel the same way, of course. But this housing situation is horrible. What can we do? We'll just have to wait." Yelena gently freed herself and looking around, said brightly, "This place is a mess. It's a wonder the government hasn't closed it down completely – but what a sublime place to work. So inspiring for the artist in you, what with the willows and the silver birches, and that singing. It's as if you're being serenaded while you create. Where does it come from? Does it go on all the time?"

Sasha smiled, "I think you're trying to distract me," he said. Then his face darkened. "Believe this: I'm not being serenaded. You have no idea what we sculptors have endured here. We've been told this workshop was once a chapel dedicated to a holy woman the religious people call 'Blessed Xenia.' Her devotees, mostly just silly old *babushkas,*⁺ aren't too happy about it being turned into a workshop but can't do much about it. So, they've been continuously harassing us since we first arrived. Things are a little better the last week or so, though. The authorities finally stepped in and took control of the situation. Now, instead of tearing down our signs and hiding our tools, they sing. Apparently there's no ordinance against singing. Yet."

"It's very beautiful," a shivering Lena said softly, "almost haunting." The feeling of something oddly and poignantly familiar had returned.

"I suppose," Sasha shrugged. "If you listen closely, the song they're singing tells the story of the old woman's life. She was certifiably crazy. What they call a 'holy fool.' She gave away a fortune and walked barefoot around St. Petersburg – Leningrad, I mean, in her dead husband's army uniform, giving people important information hidden in cryptic messages. They didn't know what she was trying to tell them of course, but after some later event occurred that seemed to have something to do with what she'd been saying, they insisted that she had prophesied it."

"Hard to understand such blind devotion," Yelena said. "Simple ignorance, I suppose. A good reminder to me of why education is so important. Didn't you tell me once, that your grandmother had you baptized?"

Sasha gave a harsh chuckle. Reaching down he picked up a rock, squeezing it in his hand, veins bulging along the muscles in his forearm.

"Yes, she did. And what good did it do? I'm an atheist and a communist. Which proves that holy water is nothing more than a construction of hydrogen and oxygen molecules after all." He pitched the rock across the grounds, aiming at the wooden fence. The old fence groaned as the rock thudded against it.

⁺ Familiar title for an old woman; grandmother.

Yelena didn't like the look on his face. She'd seen it before and it made her uneasy. She understood the psychological nature of religious belief and was unperturbed by it. After all, she was a medical doctor, a scientist. But for Sasha it seemed to go deeper, made him angry in some way. She changed the subject.

"Sasha, have you noticed the White Nights are here? No streetlights tonight. Very romantic. The Italian lovers can sing all they want about their full moons. Give me a *bella noche!*" Yelena walked down the wooded path and seated herself on a low stone bench, motioning for Sasha to join her. He slid across the bench and she leaned into his shoulder. The setting was idyllic. The dappled light filtering through the dense tree-cover jeweled everything it touched with iridescent mother-of-pearl. Lacking a sunset, however, it was easy to lose track of time.

"Sasha!" Yelena said, suddenly. "There went the last bus!"

CHAPTER II

Saint Petersburg 1727

They say that when a great event happens, God manifests His glory and splendor by giving the world a celestial show. This particular winter night was certainly one of those divine and majestic nights. The frosty midnight sky, instead of being its usual steely gray, glowed brilliantly with all the vibrant colors of a summer rainbow. The kaleidoscope of red, green, violet and orange beams which burst from the horizon were dancing and embracing one another in a way that was rarely, if ever, seen in Saint Petersburg. Indeed, the display unfolding in the heavens that night was quite extraordinary and surely it would be a night to remember.

The wide and immaculately clean avenue, the *Nevsky Prospekt*, with its impressive double row of trees on each side, allowed revelers a full view of the rare heavenly spectacle. Peter the Great had seen to every possible detail when creating his great city. Built on what was formerly swampland, he made St. Petersburg into one of the most impressive cities of Europe.

Tonight, the trees and streets of the city were covered with a thick blanket of snow, but the landscape didn't prevent a few drunken revelers that still lingered about from noticing what was transpiring in the heavens above them. Looking up, and trying hard to keep their balance as they slid on the icy cobblestones, they gasped in amazement at the show which was unfolding before their very eyes. Surely, the sky had never been as vibrant and as brilliant as it was that night.

The drunken men did not know that they were witnessing the phenomenon known as the Northern Lights – the great aurora in all its majesty – all they knew was that they were looking at something mystically amazing, something which also left each one of them with a foreboding sense of fear.

"What could it possibly mean?" one of them asked the others, as he tried to get a foothold.

"Hmmm...must be the announcement of some great event; but what kind of event?" asked the second one of the party. "These lights must be some kind of omen," he finished in a hushed tone, a detectable tremble in his voice.

The other men, tottering in the frost, nodded in agreement.

The third member of the drunken party, trying hard to keep his hand from shaking, began to mumble with a voice that was barely audible:

"We have not seen anything like this since the death of our Tsar Peter two years ago. But even then, it was not at all like what we are seeing now. What is it? What kind of sign can this be?"

They all shook their heads while looking at each other and it was obvious that the jolt of fear they felt was quickly sobering them up. Of course none of the men wished to be seen as cowards, but with these questions circling about in their minds and the sense of spiritual awe permeating their souls, they were compelled to act upon the significance of that moment. One by one, each man fell to the frozen ground making a full prostration, in the "old style" of the Orthodox. And with profound reverence, they crossed themselves, hoping that by doing so they would ward off whatever catastrophe they feared might occur. Then turning to the Eastern sky, they all prayed to the Mother of God, as one, for protection, using the prayers they had learned as children.

The revelers were indeed shaken with the spectacular event, as were others that happened to see it that special night. What they had all failed to notice as they gazed upon the Eastern sky, however, were the cries of a newborn baby coming from the very place on the *Nevsky Prospect* where they had first stopped. The baby's cries came from one of the new brick homes on the banks of the *Neva River*. They were the cries of a newborn infant named Xenia Grigorievna, who would one day become a saint, and who would also have a great impact not only on the city of Saint Petersburg, but on all of Russia.

The impact she would have would not be simply a temporal one, as had been assumed by those witnessing the aurora of that night, but something far greater – for it was to be a spiritual one as well. It was a combination that would see the land of Russia rise to an almost unheard of prominence. For as long as Saint Xenia prayed, and for as long as Saint Xenia roamed the cold, damp streets of Saint Petersburg, Russia would be richly blessed by God.

◆❋❋❋◆

It had been two years now since the Tsar, known as Peter the Great, had died. He chose the *Neva River*, which lays at the head of the Gulf of Finland on the Baltic Sea to bring his vision of a great imperial Russian city to reality – a city which would rival the great cities of Europe. St. Petersburg, as it would be known, was built on marshes, partially on land and partially on water, and it was crisscrossed with canals whose banks were consolidated by rows of stakes and then lined with splendid red granite.

Peter the Great had the well-designed plans for his new city executed beautifully. He made sure that all the main streets were paved, and since that area of Russia did not have much indigenous stone, he had every merchant ship entering the city include stones with their cargo. Peter envisioned a city which would look much like Amsterdam, with canals and waterways running throughout: the Venice of the North.

New homes were also being built for the people who would inhabit the city, and they were located in specially designated areas known as the Millionaya, the Luguvaya, and the English Quay. Peter wanted an architectural style completely different from the traditional wooden homes of Russia, so he brought over architects from Italy, craftsmen skilled in design who would ensure the Western European flair he craved.

Indeed, the beautiful and elegant brick and stone homes which characterized much of St. Petersburg originally, were reminiscent of those traditionally found in lands which lay further south. They were not fully suitable to the cold climate of the Russian north. Yet, despite their drafty interiors, these stately homes managed to form an opulent and picturesque scene that was notably impressive.

Behind the splendid veneer of decadence, however, lay hidden neighborhoods of the most wretched wooden huts one could possibly imagine, constructed on the frozen and muddied unpaved streets of the city. Here, lived the poor unfortunate laborers, the invisible force who not only built St. Petersburg with their hands, but who also maintained this great new city each and every day with their never-resting toil.

Included in the plans he made for his city, Tsar Peter also designated the quality of home an individual would live in according to his station in life: thus, the higher an individual's social status, the better his house and neighborhood. Since the baby, Xenia Grigorievna was the daughter of a *dvoryanin*[+] her home was made of brick and was beautifully covered with stucco.

Although Saint Xenia's mother and father now lived in the grand new city and a lovely new home, they still longed to one day return to their ancestral home. They often lamented, as did others, that they had been forced to move so that Tsar Peter could populate his new city. However, as wistful as they may have been, it was little compared to the unfortunate peasant laborers who had been relocated to work there without partaking of the plenty.

Tens of thousands of peasants had been forced to migrate across Russia, marching hundreds of miles through frozen land. Tens of thousands died on the way, and tens of thousands more died in the harsh conditions of this artificial city that was located far from any sustainable natural food source. All in all, it has been estimated that one million people died so that Tsar Peter could build the city of Saint Petersburg, his "Window to the West."

The pitiable souls that managed to survive despite the grueling ordeals inhabited despicable huts in the poorest neighborhoods of St. Petersburg. The worst of these were found in and around the vicinity of Saint Matthias Parish – the *Petersburgskaya Storona*. It was here that Saint Xenia would spend the last thirty-seven years of her adult life, ministering with her Christ-like love and prayers to the people that needed her most.

[+] A nobleman.

CHAPTER III

Leningrad, 1963

The trip to Sasha's workplace had become routine. Leaving *Mariinsky Hospital* by 7:00 p.m. most evenings, as she had done tonight, Yelena would catch the bus at the corner of *Litenyy Avenue* and *Nevsky Prospekt* and ride it to the *Smolensk Cathedral*. Only 10.5 kilometers, the journey often included a long wait at the bus stop, sometimes an hour or more. The route included numerous stops along the way and she often didn't arrive there until 9:00 p.m., or later. Since the last bus returning home left the stop in front of the cathedral at 10:30, the time she spent with Sasha was dear.

This evening, as she waited with the small crowd that had gathered to take advantage of Leningrad's public transportation service (however poor it might be), a vendor dressed like an English tourist in a driving cap and threadbare tweed jacket wheeled his little tanker of *kvass*[+]

[+] A beer-like drink made from rye bread.

over, parking it on the sidewalk close to the group. Yelena hadn't eaten since breakfast and gladly paid him for a cup. She drank deeply, feeling immediately rejuvenated by the sour, fermented liquid.

"Please," a voice rasped behind her, "for the sake of Christ, have pity on a couple of poor beggars?"

Turning toward the voice, Yelena spied a middle-aged man with ragged pants held up by a dirty length of rope. One leg of his trousers was superfluous, tied off at the knee with string. He leaned on a crude homemade crutch looking at her, and gestured to another beggar with striking eyes who sat nearby, silently looking on, an open hat in his lap to catch spare coins tossed their way.

"We're just going to *Khram Spasa na Krovi*."[+] He lisped the words through snaggled, rotting teeth, his tangled mustache bobbing. "But we could use a cup of strength to help us finish the journey."

Yelena rummaged in her purse and took out two coins. She paid the *kvass* vendor with one, passed a cup to each beggar, and put the other coin in the poor man's hat. When he raised his head to thank her and Yelena looked into his startling green eyes, she had the curious feeling she'd seen the man somewhere before. Perhaps he was often in the area begging and she'd seen him without registering his face.

"Give me your name, sister," the seated man said quietly, "I'll mention it when I pray to our Savior."

Yelena drained her cup and handed it back to the vendor, tossing an answer over her shoulder. "You don't

---

[+] Church of the Savior on Spilt Blood. A famous cathedral in St. Petersburg built on the site where Emperor Alexander II was killed in March 1881.

need to do that," she said, with an indulgent smile, moving back toward the bus stop crowd, "Enjoy your *kvass*, comrades, and good luck to you."

◆❋❋❋◆

A heated argument had been fermenting for days between two route-regulars of late middle-age and had ripened fully while Yelena was away. Both men were bricklayers, their creased faces still dusty from a day on the job. One man, short and stocky with stiff salt-and-pepper hair that arched between his ears like a grizzled rooster's comb, was defending the strategy employed by his favorite chess-player in the Leningrad City Tournament. The other man, slight for a bricklayer but wiry, with a wide, intellectual brow and intense brown eyes, shook his head in disbelief.

"I pity you, Vadim, my friend. Only a fool would defend such a fateful move. Your man lost. Or have you forgotten?"

"He was rattled. The whole time he was planning his final move, he was distracted by the rumor."

"What rumor is that?"

"The rumor that Constantin Mikhailovich Klaman entered the tournament illegally. I've heard it said that he isn't even a native. Some claim he's actually a Swede, smuggled into Leningrad as a teenager so he could learn to play chess like a Russian."

The slender man had seemed like the mellower of the two. Now he bristled visibly and the waiting bus patrons pressed close to hear what he would say next, or perhaps to see if fists would be used. He stuck out his chest and made as if to speak, but no words were formed. He simply took a long, deep breath and turned away. The crowd parted to let him through.

Someone had sighted the bus approaching and the group moved forward together, lining up like schoolchildren to board the dilapidated vehicle. The rear of the bus filled up first. Yelena took a window seat behind the driver and laid her head against the blurry glass, watching the bus stop disappear behind them. The smaller of the quibbling chess enthusiasts had the seat next to her. Yelena scooted toward the wall of the bus so he could make room for a sturdy *babushka* wearing mudboots and a plastic rain-bonnet to squeeze by with her basket of leeks. Sagging into the back of his seat with an audible sigh the man rested his disproportionately long, sinewy arms on his chest. Yelena looked over at him. She couldn't help asking, "Why didn't you have the last word? You could have, you know."

The man shrugged his shoulders. "You've heard the expression 'a fly can't get into a closed mouth?' Well, my mother used to say it to me often when I was a lad. I'm forty-three now. After thirty-odd years of choking on flies, I smartened up and took her advice."

"You knew the whole time that he was making that up to get you going, didn't you?"

The bricklayer grinned. White brick dust disappeared into the deep crevices around his mouth. His dark eyes took on a boyish, rascally gleam. "Kostik Mikhailovich is a third cousin of mine, twice removed," he said. "Our ancestors laid the first bricks in St. Petersburg. He's as Russian, and as native to Leningrad, as anyone can possibly be."

Yelena arched her eyebrows, smiling, then turned her gaze out the window.

The bus passed by the beggars who had finished their *kvass*. The lame one supported by his quiet companion, they were hobbling down the street toward the Church of the Savior on Spilt Blood.

"Look at that," her seat companion said with disgust, "how do they sleep at night, knowing that we comrades are doing their part?"

Yelena didn't answer. How could she? – guilty as she was

of encouraging parasites. She was resigned to her weakness for beggars. If treating the indigent and needy like ticks on a dog was the mark of a good citizen, Yelena knew she would always fall short of Soviet perfection.

Suddenly, Yelena realized where she'd seen that face. Cleaned up, the seated beggar could have sat in as a double for any portrait of Alexander II, the tsar-reformer who had finally freed Russia's serfs. Just as he was set to grant the people a constitution, that same tsar had been assassinated by impatient liberal activists on the very spot where his look-alike, the beggar, was headed to pray now.

Yelena recalled the story from her school history lessons. The Tsar was travelling in a carriage along the Catherine Canal with an armed Cossack in the seat beside him and six more on horseback, when members of a radical group called The People's Will tossed bombs at his carriage. Missing the Tsar, the bombs landed in the group of Cossacks. Tsar Alexander insisted on getting out of the carriage to give aid to his men, and it was at that moment that one of the activists, Ignatei Grinevitsky, lobbed yet another bomb. The blast from the explosion was so great that it killed not only the Tsar, but his assassin as well.

The magnificent Church of the Savior, the jewel of St. Petersburg (now Leningrad) with its marble and mosaics, was built on the patch of ground stained by the "spilt blood" of Alexander II. Not only his blood, however, but also the blood of his loyal Cossack guards, and of the assassin (portrayed as a hero in Yelena's history classes) who finally succeeded in killing the emperor of Russia.   Yelena mused that despite their considerable progress, the city's cathedrals still held sway in the minds and hearts of its inhabitants, with their stories and incense.

As her bus crossed the canal, heading toward a different cathedral, Yelena removed the beggars from her thoughts with purposeful effort, feeling her mood lighten as though a satchel loaded with books had been taken off her shoulders. Sasha had accused her on more than one occasion of having more on her mind than simply seeing him when she visited. He was teasing of course, but he was not entirely wrong in his accusation. She wondered how he sensed that the place captivated her so thoroughly. It wasn't just the majesty of the *Smolensky Cathedral*, or the quaint little chapel-workshop, or the melancholy loveliness of the cemetery; the place held a deep, mysterious allure for Yelena that thrilled and concerned her both at the same time.

◆❘✽❘✽❘✽❘◆

Sasha was waiting near the steps of the cathedral when the bus pulled up and Yelena and the other passengers unboarded. He stood off a little way from the entrance to avoid the beggars draped like seaweed over the church steps. Across the country all but a baker's dozen churches had been closed to worshipers. *Smolensk Cathedral* was no exception, but judging from the crowds, a whole slew of Leningrad's unfortunates apparently hadn't heard the news.

Catching sight of Yelena, Sasha gave a hearty wave, nearly breaking into a run as he strode toward her. His arms were as unyielding as tree trunks as he wrapped her in a tight embrace and then took her by the elbow, steering her toward the cemetery and his workshop. As they wound their way across the grounds to the chapel, Yelena's heart was re-pierced by the sight of the broken crosses lying about the cemetery.

"Sasha, who's responsible for all of these broken crosses?"

"*Komosols.*⁺ Communist hooligans." Sasha said bitterly, shaking his head. "In such a frenzy they couldn't appreciate

---

⁺ All-Union Lenin Communist Youth League. A selective Communist party organization for children 14-28 years old.

that these crosses were just outdated religious symbols – they were works of art; too dense to understand that we don't have to destroy all evidence of the past in order to build a future."

Yelena sent Sasha a sharp, questioning look. "But surely some art had to be destroyed in order to counteract the opiate nature of religion. It's like blotting out the memory of a narcotic drug. The *Komosols* must have known that such monuments would be a constant reminder to ignorant believers of what they must give up," Yelena said, with more intensity than she felt, trying to rid herself of the depressed feeling she got from looking at the graves.

Sasha smiled at Yelena's heated reply. "You're absolutely right, I'm sure," he said, slipping an arm around her waist. "Since that's exactly what we've been told to think. But personally, I have a hard time tolerating destruction in any form, for any reason. It runs against my creative grain."

Unconvinced, Yelena pressed on, though she could not have said why she wished to argue the point. "You know as well as I do, that in order for a government to make progress, drastic measures have to be taken sometimes." Opening the door to the workshop, Sasha ushered Yelena in, keeping his hand on the small of her back. She glanced around the room and up to the vaulted ceiling.

"Look around, Sasha. Here's an illustration of what I've been saying. You've told me this chapel was once ornately decorated, the walls and ceiling covered by masterful icons and religious art. No doubt all of it was paid for by the nobility, but what currency did they use? I'll tell you. It was the sweat and toil of the poor peasants who worked the land."

"That's where you're wrong, sweetheart," Sasha said, striding to the center of the room, turning his eyes up to the denuded ceiling as if seeing the original frescoes and architecture.

"It was the people themselves who gave the money. Originally, there was just a small chapel over Xenia's tomb. In 1902, it was they who paid for this beautiful building. I'm just glad it wasn't razed after the Revolution, like so many others. I understand what you're saying, but in my mind what you're describing amounts to a necessary evil."

Gesturing toward the cemetery he said, "And I can't help believing that much of the destruction was unnecessary." He shrugged, "What can I say? I am an artist after all!"

◆❉◆❉◆❉◆

Thoughts of Sasha occupied Yelena's mind as she boarded the bus to go home. Leaving him was becoming more and more difficult with each visit and he never tried to hide his impatience to make her his wife.

What would it really be like to live together as a married couple? she thought to herself dreamily. *To share not just romantic stolen moments, but the struggle of day to day living?* Sasha was strong, and dependable. He also loved her with all his passionate artist's heart. She knew that was true. But furthermore, he also possessed a sensitive intelligence – a trait she had not found in ready supply among the men she had known previously – and one which she found most endearing.

Just before Yelena left, Sasha had given her a lesson in iconography, telling her about the images that had once graced the chapel. He explained the difference between an ordinary painting and an icon as being one of purpose. Painting an icon, he told her, is more like writing a prayer than creating a work of art. Its purpose is spiritual, to transport the beholder through the depicted image to another realm. The icon "writer" prays as he paints, believing that an angel directs his hand.

Yelena had watched Sasha carefully as he talked, sensing that he warmed to the subject in a special way. But when he saw that she was studying his face the light went out in Sasha's eyes as quickly as if he'd drawn a curtain. His expression abruptly changed to one of scorn.

Yelena understood why. With Kruschev at the helm of government, things had eased up considerably for artists, but one couldn't be too careful, especially when touching on religious subjects. Even an art history lesson might be misconstrued by an eavesdropper. If Sasha were accused of this and his explanation rejected, he could be labeled an enemy of the State and barred from the Union of Artists.

In the moments before Sasha brought them both back to reality, Yelena had been experiencing something similar to the feelings shown by the fire in Sasha's eyes. The workshop chapel and the stories about Saint Xenia had a nostalgic effect on her, bringing to mind a somewhat golden childhood. A childhood that included bed-time stories told by her foster mother, a woman who was the epitome of love and kindness. Vague, forgotten memories floated back into her line of inner sight, like dandelion seeds on a breeze: green fields and flowers; mushroom hunting among the firs and larches; sweet scents drifting on the night air; candles and hymns and chants; and bells ringing in the early light.

It wasn't exactly a decadent past to be put aside for an "enlightened" future. In fact, when Yelena dared allow herself to think about it, she found the social climate of Leningrad to be cold and indifferent by comparison. And she felt that something inside of her had cooled as well. It was one of those necessary evils Sasha had mentioned on occasion. In her case, Yelena knew, it was necessary to wall off those scenes from her memory, to suppress the past when it threatened to interfere with her future.

CHAPTER IV

Saint Petersburg 1727-1753

Adorable baby Xenia was one of the prettiest and sweetest baby girls the *babushkas* of St. Petersburg had gazed their weary eyes upon in quite some time. Even the most hardened and embittered old woman smiled upon meeting this charming creature. She had a wonderful disposition, rarely crying, but always smiling and taking delight in everything around her. As a young child, she had an extraordinary capacity for love. Her young heart felt a special type of empathy for any suffering, whether it was another child or an animal. In fact, if her mother had not scolded her from time to time in order to curb her attempts at trying to help everyone and everything, their home would have become not only a menagerie, but also a homeless shelter.

Xenia was also gifted with a profound spiritual

understanding that was rare in a child of her young age, and though her mother acknowledged this as a gift from God, she couldn't help but be somewhat concerned by it. A mother's love is limitless; and it was this great love that made her fear her sweet daughter's purity of heart might cause little Xenia pain and suffering someday. Her mother would ultimately be proven correct in this. But the trials would also be manifest as God's divine will.

In time, Xenia grew up to be a pleasing young lady. The innate kindness within her heart and soul gave Xenia a beauty beyond the physical features, a beauty which radiated virtue, making her even more attractive as the years went on. Such beauty coupled with such a lovely disposition, could not possibly go unnoticed in St. Petersburg for long! It was only a matter of time before she attracted the eye of the handsome and eligible young colonel, Andrei Theodorovich Petrov. Not only was the young gentleman gifted with an honorific position, but also with a spirited and fun-loving nature.

Andrei Theodorovich Petrov was an officer in the famed and renowned *Preobrazhensky Regiment*, an elite company founded by Peter the Great for the St. Petersburg's nobility. Being an esteemed member of this distinguished corps, handsome Andrei was given the title of colonel at a relatively young age. In addition to this great honor and its accompanying privileges, the personable Andrei was the opportune beneficiary of an even higher distinction. Because he was blessed with a voice of great loveliness, and because his deep baritone chants had so enthralled the Empress Elizabeth, he was bestowed with the privilege of being one of her Imperial Choristers.

As a young child, Xenia had always been intrigued by Andrei, noting his talent, liveliness and impressive bearing as he sang for his school: the Noble Cadet Corp. As the years passed and she reached adolescence, Xenia watched him admiringly as he made deep bows during his presentations to Empress Elizabeth. Dressed in his full regalia with its gold trim glittering brightly on the red and green uniform, Xenia was awestruck, and with the extra tributes that were now being commended him, the young St. Petersburg girls considered him a fine catch indeed.

As to be expected, Andrei and Xenia soon fell in love. They were formally betrothed, and would shortly thereafter be married in the majestic Cathedral of Saints Peter and Paul. Like most young couples in love, they waited impatiently and in nervous anticipation of their upcoming wedding and the Holy Mystery of Crowning which would be performed in the beautiful Russian Orthodox service.

When the day finally arrived, the sun was shining bright and the blue sky was without a cloud. In the church, the presiding bishop glowed resplendently in his gilded robe as he waited for the couple to approach the impressive altar with its high and ornate iconostasis. It was there, with all the customary pomp and pageantry of the Russian Orthodox Church, that he performed the ancient matrimonial sacrament; they both felt lovingly enveloped in the Orthodox Church's solemn and sacred blessings.[+]

While Xenia absorbed the spiritual depth of the hymns being chanted, as the nuptial crowns were being held above her head in the ancient ritual, she started to pray silently. "Dear Lord," she said. "Help me to be everything that Andrei needs and wants." Xenia was silently thanking the Lord for this gift of love He had blessed her with, and she

---

[+] In the Orthodox Church, marriage is much more than merely a private transaction between two individuals; it is a sacred event in which Jesus Christ Himself participates through the presence of the sacramental minister, who is the Priest, and of the praying community, the Church. It is also considered a "great mystery," because it is the mystery of the meeting of human love and divine love, the very sign and image of God's presence with humanity.

promised Him that with every ounce of her being she would dedicate herself to the welfare of her beloved husband for the rest of their lives.

The promise that Xenia made on that memorable day of her wedding would prove to be more far-reaching than she could have imagined. With each year that passed, Xenia's love and admiration for Andrei grew stronger and stronger, and they were fast becoming as close as a couple can be. They lived harmoniously and peacefully, fully enjoying each other's company. The eventual passing of Xenia's immediate family drew them even closer together, as Andrei became all the family that Xenia had left in the world.

In their first years of marriage, young Xenia would attend all the joyous and elegant fêtes and dinners that they were invited to, in order to be with her beloved husband. As long as Xenia was with Andrei, she enjoyed herself, wherever they went. Because she had great love and respect for the royal family, and most especially for the Grand Duchess Catherine, she was especially thrilled when the royal court was in attendance at these events. On such occasions, Xenia often found herself thinking with admiration: *How devout Catherine is; she is seen at church praying quite often.*

As she and Andrei were having their breakfast of black bread, cheese and tea one morning after yet another gala event, Xenia brought up the subject of the Grand Duchess Catherine to him. She was curious to know more about her, so she asked him what he had heard. Andrei put down his cup of tea and said, "Well, I have heard that everyone at court, most especially the royal guards, but also the foreign dignitaries, know Catherine to be exceptionally knowledgeable, compassionate and attentive to all her attendants. I think that she will truly make a fine Empress someday." Xenia nodded her head in agreement and smiled.

With her most beloved husband, the dashing and handsome colonel at her side, Xenia's first years of marriage were positively delightful. While she was not one who enjoyed the gossip and intrigues of social circles, she was, never the less, respected and liked by all whom she met because of her sweet and considerate disposition. Eventually, it was inevitable that the exciting social life they experienced would start to disturb her spiritual nature, especially when she began to hear the whispered remarks around her about indiscretions going on at the parties of Empress Elizabeth. This type of talk and gossip dismayed her greatly. *Surely all these things cannot be true*, she thought. She kept these doubts to herself, however, and never questioned Andrei about them, since she found such talk too shameful and unbelievable to discuss.

With the glitter fading away from Xenia's initial years of awe and excitement about court life, she found herself increasingly upset by the undeniable excesses and vanities of the Empress Elizabeth. While her soul refrained from judging what she saw, she couldn't help but feel uncomfortable; it contrasted so greatly with the poverty she noticed all around her which tugged at her heart more and more strongly. While some have the ability to overlook that which is distasteful around them, young Xenia could not do so. For her, poverty and suffering were not distasteful matters, but rather real life situations that she increasingly wanted to alleviate.

The harshest circumstances in St. Petersburg were concentrated around the *Petersburgskaya Storona*, the poorest area of the city, and it distressed Xenia the most. The inhabitants of this area were in such dire need, that even the simplest piece of bread was a rarity for them. Their diets consisted of nothing more than roots and cabbage.

While stories whirled around about how proud the Empress Elizabeth was of her fifteen thousand Parisian gowns and her five thousand pairs of shoes, and of her great extravagance in having the palace's many outdoor statues gilded, Xenia would not allow herself to think ill of an Empress that was anointed at her coronation. Imperfect though she may be, Xenia knew that the Empress had been sanctified by God. Despite the fact that her outrageous vanities were obvious to all, Xenia also knew that the Empress was exceptionally generous to her court. "Dear Lord God, how I wish our Empress would also extend her generosity to the poor of Saint Petersburg," Xenia sighed, with a heavy heart, in her daily prayers.

Soon, Xenia began to hear even more disturbing accusations circulated about the Royal Family. Though she tried very hard to dismiss such conversations, she could not avoid them all together at the events which she and Andrei attended. Xenia always found something good to say and believe about everyone, and ignored the unfounded gossip she heard, but one evening when the whisperings had reached a particular level of frenzy, she was appalled to find herself weighing the possibility of their truth. "No, no, it cannot be true! Elizabeth is the daughter of Peter the Great, and besides that, she is also the Holy Empress of all of the Russias – the anointed Tsarina, and head of the Holy Russian Orthodox Church," she reassured herself.

One day, as Andrei and Xenia were walking home on a mild spring morning after attending the Divine Liturgy at church, she couldn't help but blurt out to him, "Andrei, I am really quite shocked at how malicious people can be!"

"Xenia, whatever are you referring to, dearest? I have rarely, if ever, heard you sound so upset."

"How can they say these things about our Sovereign? Don't they know that she has been chosen and sanctified by God to be the Empress of all the Russias, and of the Russian Orthodox Church?"

"Don't be so appalled my dear, and ignore what people

say," was Andrei's only response to her. He loved his wife's innocence and religious piety, and he didn't want to say anything further that might upset her. He had great respect for Xenia's inability to conceive of worldly selfishness and immorality of any sort, so rather than scandalize her, he decided that it was best not to disturb her peace of mind with the sad truths of human weakness. He noticed that her thoughts were, in fact, turning more and more to God in prayer recently.

It was true. Xenia had been begging the Holy Mother of God to intercede with her Son, in the hopes that they would be blessed with a child.

"My dearest Mother of God," she prayed each day. "I know that we must accept whatever God's will is for us, but it pains me greatly not to be able to give my beloved Andrei children, especially a son, who would one day be able to join him as an officer in the noble regiment that he is so proud of. Please give us that blessing, for you know that my only desire in this world is to obey my Lord Jesus, and to make my Andrei happy."

Meanwhile, the partying and carousing at the royal court continued, and soon it would adversely affect Andrei and Xenia far more harmfully than by just hearing gossip. The Empress was now requesting that in addition to Andrei singing at her public fêtes and dinners, he also sing at her own private parties as well. Making matters even worse, the Grand Duke Peter, who was the Empress Elizabeth's nephew and future heir, became more and demanding of Andrei's time and company, too.

The Grand Duke Peter was known for his childish Prussian war games and for private drinking parties during which his guests enjoyed musical entertainments and behaved riotously. At the Grand Duke's command, the officers of the Royal Guard were expected to attend, and of all the Royal Guards, Andrei's company was the most desired by the future Emperor and Tsar of all the Russias. Andrei, therefore, was obliged to attend all his parties, not only because of the pleasure which his singing voice gave as entertainment, but also because the Grand Duke genuinely enjoyed his amiable and fun-loving nature. There was no way out for Andrei that he could see. He certainly didn't want to disappoint his superiors. And if he didn't obey as expected, he was afraid there could be dire consequences.

Xenia was perplexed. She didn't know the full extent of carousing which went on at the palace, but noted a sad change in Andrei, who became increasingly despondent and detached, sometimes flying into bouts of anger which greatly disturbed her. Since Andrei hid the details from her out of respect for her pious nature, she could not understand what had caused her husband to change.

"If only we had a child, maybe the Royal Family wouldn't be so demanding of his time," she thought sadly, for Xenia was now almost twenty-six years old, and had not yet been able to conceive. She believed that Andrei desperately needed to become a father in order for him to become more responsible and mature. Since she was not able to give him a child, she felt that she was solely to blame for his worldly excesses.

Xenia spent hours praying to God to conceive a child, but it was to no avail. It was simply not our Lord's will to give Xenia and Andrei this blessing. In time, however, the spiritual blessings that He would bestow on Xenia would be far greater than that which she prayed for. Through Xenia's many personal sacrifices, the Lord would not only give His spiritual blessings to her and Andrei, but ultimately, to the tens of thousands of souls in Saint Petersburg and all of Russia, souls that would, in time, turn to Him and embrace Him through the intercessions of His chosen and beloved servant: Saint Xenia of Saint Petersburg.

CHAPTER V

Leningrad, 1963

It was June and the days were mild and pleasant. Yelena usually greeted nature's rebirth with enthusiasm. Lately, though, the scents and sounds of summer only made the hours she spent inside the olive-drab walls of *Mariinsky Hospital* more difficult to bear.

At the start of her medical career, Yelena had been full of naive hope. Hope in herself and her freshly acquired stock of knowledge; hope in the Soviet scientists who were making new discoveries; hope that those scientists would soon be finding cures for the diseases that shortened her young patients' lives and robbed the nation of potentially productive citizens. Hope had slowly declined into resignation, however, as the reality of the limited means she had to work with began to sink in.

As a student she had been taught that the individual patient was the concern of society as a whole, and that unlike capitalist countries where only the rich could afford to be well, when a Soviet citizen became ill the government would do something about it. But what she saw played out in the wards of her own hospital told her that this ideal was yet hanging far out of reach.

In 1933, a medical commission from the West had been given a store-front tour of the Soviet health care system and reported back in glowing terms. They'd fully bought the picture painted by their hosts of peaceful rest homes for workers in need of recuperation, and modern hospitals equipped with the most recent technology. These, of course, were staffed with unusually competent doctors and nurses whose goal was to provide the best medicine, without care for profit. Idealistic medical students like Yelena were brought up on gilded accounts of those commissions much as young worker bees are fed on nectar.

While she couldn't allow herself to think of them as propaganda, such reports contrasted sharply with the dingy truth that was the Soviet health care system as Yelena knew it: a system she tried hard to convince herself was simply experiencing growing pains. Surely, someday soon those accounts would be a reality.

Affecting a smile and straightening her cap, Yelena pushed open the door to Ward #10. Beginning her morning rounds, she met up with Evgenia, the stocky ward matron, who suffered from an overactive thyroid which was insufficiently treated by the endocrinologist she'd been assigned. Her greenish eyes bulged and darted, and coarse dark hairs sprouted like porcupine quills from her chin. She pulled Yelena briskly aside as she stepped into the ward, informing her curtly that the daughter of a high-ranking Party member had been admitted last night and should be seen first thing.

Despite her appearance, which made her seem severe, Evgenia was a decent person. She was often moody with the staff, but the Ward #10 patients knew her to be a jolly nurse; that is, when she wasn't in a panic about caring for the sick children of important Party officials.

Yelena glanced over to the bed indicated by the nervous matron. A slight girl of eight or nine lay with her eyes closed. She was listening, or giving the appearance of listening, to a woman dressed far too warmly for the day, in a smart yellow suit trimmed in fox fur, reading aloud from a book of folk stories.

Yelena recognized the book; it was one of those sanitized re-tellings of old peasant tales – the kind published under Stalin in an attempt to purge Soviet children's literature of romanticism. The goal of these new books was to remind youngsters of how miserable life was in pre-Revolutionary Russia. Next to beloved traditional characters like *Vasilissa the Fair*, *Petrushka the Puppet* and the ultra-evil *Kaschei the Immortal*, the Soviet versions were pathetically prudish. They hadn't been well-received by children in the 1940's and 1950's, and judging by the bored look on the girl's face, the situation hadn't changed much since Yelena was young.

Stopping by the bed closest to the door, Yelena bent and felt the forehead of another patient, a blond five year old. His skin was burning hot. She kept her expression cheerful, nevertheless.

"*Privyet,*[+] Nikolai! And how is my little soldier today?"

"Not so good, Doctor. I threw up three times already this morning."

God loves trinity. Yelena was only slightly disturbed to hear the voice of her foster mother stating the old proverb so clearly in her head. It had been happening a lot lately and she was starting to get used to it. Looking into Nikolai's face she was brought back to reality in an instant. The poor boy was white as a sturgeon's belly, and his hazel eyes were glazed with fever.

"I'll send a nurse in with something for your tummy. Do you hurt anywhere?" Yelena took Nikolai's hand and moved

---

[+] Informal greeting; i.e. hi, hey.

his wrist lightly. "How does that feel?"

He winced. "It hurts a little."

"And that?" Pressing the knee joint, Yelena manipulated Nikolai's leg, checking for stiffness.

Though he made no sound, Yelena knew her stoic patient was feeling pain as he drew in a breath and set his mouth. Finishing her exam and taking up his chart, Yelena made some notes while Nikolai dozed off in a fitful slumber interrupted by jerks of pain and low moans. As she turned to go, he opened his eyes.

"You missed seeing *Babushka* again, Doctor. She was here this morning."

Yelena smiled. "We will meet, I promise. Your *babushka* spends a lot of time here I'm told. We're bound to cross paths soon."

◆❙✱❙✱❙✱❙◆

The next seven hours were busy ones, giving Yelena time for thoughts of little else except her patients. Later that evening however, as she got off the bus at her building, one of those pre-revolution structures in the city center that had been converted into apartments long ago, she was thinking of Nikolai and the odd memory that had flashed into her mind as he spoke. Absentmindedly, she climbed the stairs to the two-room flat she shared with a bickering, on-again-off-again couple who, lucky for her, both worked the night shift.

Vanya and Irena were a slovenly pair. The first thing Yelena did when she arrived home every evening was to set about cleaning up the mess they invariably left behind when they rushed off to work. Tonight they had left the remains of their dinner on the table, and what looked like a pile of dirty laundry on the sofa.

She ran the sink full of hot water, tossed in a spoonful of soap flakes and put the dirty dishes to soak. Scooping up the pile of clothing, she opened the door to the apartment's only bedroom and dumped it unceremoniously on the floor, reclosing the door behind her. She straightened the sofa cushions, watered a potted wax begonia that Irena had been very proud of buying but had since neglected, and went to find something to eat.

After a dinner of pickled mushrooms and sliced bread with three cups of strong tea, Yelena opened the door to her small, cramped closet and chose a simple black skirt and a cream colored sweater. Both items were getting on in age, but still passable for an evening out. Though she would have liked a dress in a print or a bright summer color, she had neither the time nor the energy for standing on line for hours in the off-chance that she would be lucky enough to buy one – and she had no *babushka* to do it for her as many working girls did. Teasing her hair a little on the crown and brushing her bangs smooth, she pulled her hair back into a ponytail and tied it with a black velvet ribbon.

Forcing her tired feet into a pair of ill-fitting low-heeled sandals, Yelena was distracted by a sudden realization. Ever since she first visited Sasha's workshop, snatches of long forgotten conversations and scraps of buried memories had been finding their way into her thoughts unbidden. Some of those memories were benign: chickens and flowers and sunny summer days, but others were more dangerous: hymns heard from the folds of her mother's skirt, candlelit churches and prayers chanted by bearded priests. Perhaps she had underestimated the nostalgic effect the singing she'd heard at *Smolensky Cemetery* had on her.

According to their prior arrangement, Sasha met her at 8:00 p.m. on *Bolshaya Morskaya Street* in front of the House of the Union of Artists. She was impressed, seeing him on the sidewalk, by how ruggedly handsome her fiancé was. Most often now, she saw him at his workshop. They rarely met outside of it.

"Wow. You look wonderful," he said.

"You think so? I was just thinking the same about you. I know I shouldn't admit it, but I can't remember choosing this outfit. I'm afraid my mind was on other things."

"Ouch. What's so important you didn't think of me when you were getting dressed?"

"We can talk about that later. Now, tell me all about this Vladimir Gorb and why it was so important to get to his exhibition."

"I'd rather show you," Sasha grinned, taking her arm. "Let's go inside."

For the next two hours Yelena gazed at Gorb's landscapes and portraits; learning, under the careful tutelage of Sasha, about the impressionist painter who was not afraid to convey beauty as light and reflection, who had even taught the technique to his students at the Repyn Institute during a time when doing so could have gotten him expelled. Sasha was in unabashed awe of the man. He pointed to a painting done in oils titled *Woman in Black Beret*. Yelena knew nothing of art analysis, but the figure's downcast eyes and pensive expression were poignant, even to an inexperienced observer.

"This, Yelena," Sasha said, lowering his voice to a whisper, "is what Dostoevsky meant by 'beauty will save the world.'"

◆❘✳❘✳❘✳❘◆

That night, in the relative quiet of her communal apartment, Yelena dreamed of Sasha, with a black beret perched jauntily on his head, covering the walls of *Mariinsky Hospital* in brightly-colored murals.

At first the murals seemed to be landscapes with tiny *izbas*[+] and rambling fields under spacious blue skies. And

---

[+] Countryside peasant dwellings traditionally made of wood.

there were depicted peasants with fleshy noses and weathered, patient faces. But somehow as Yelena dreamed, the murals changed and now Sasha, no longer wearing an artist's beret and smock but dressed in a black robe, was using his brush to cover the dreary walls of Ward #10 with multi-colored icons. He had painted images of Christ with the most humble, tender expression and eyes that seemed to move to meet Yelena's as she watched Sasha paint them. In the dream she felt in the most natural way that the Christ of the icons loved her and that she had always somehow known it.

And there was a sprawling fresco of the six days of creation, just like the one in the church where she had worshiped as a child. In Sasha's version, zebras and elephants and whales and bears marched just over the heads of the children in their beds. And now, as she watched, he splashed the ceiling with brilliant blue paint and spritzed it with golden stars.

All the while she slept, Yelena was aware of a voice singing a melody that was faintly familiar, as if she'd heard it before in some other dream. And suddenly, there was Nikolai, holding the hand of a woman who bore a striking resemblance to Yelena's foster mother. He lifted his head from his pillow and said, "Here she is, Doctor. Here is my *babushka*."

◆❘✳❘✳❘✳❘◆

A few days later, Yelena went to the workshop to see Sasha. She was feeling troubled by the nostalgia she couldn't shake, the creeping, disloyal thoughts unbefitting a former Young Pioneer. Surely a visit with Sasha at his studio would put her right. The surroundings were so lovely, and he always knew what to say to cheer her up.

Recalling the last time she had made this visit, she smiled. She had gotten quite heated up trying to qualify the difference between the throngs of pilgrims who lined up to see Lenin's tomb and the tenacious believers who still visited Russia's closed churches and made pilgrimages to so-called holy places.

Sasha had laughed outright at her, pointing out that while Lenin may have been a god-like personage, he never claimed to actually be God, as Jesus Christ had done. And the crowds of the casually curious who visited his tomb each day bore no resemblance in Sasha's mind to the simple, stubborn believers who would rather die than denounce their faith in a God the Soviet government insisted had never existed.

◆❋❋❋◆

Intending to surprise Sasha, Yelena hadn't called ahead, and when she arrived he was nowhere to be found. Yelena, prowling around the cemetery grounds in search of her fiancé, heard singing and found herself inexplicably following it. Standing outside the chapel was a short, pleasant-faced middle-aged woman wearing a white and blue kerchief on her head.

Pulling back to stand behind a lilac bush, Yelena listened as the woman finished her song. When the last note was sung, the woman crossed herself boldly and bowed in the direction of the cathedral. Stooping by the adjacent chapel, she scooped up a handful of dirt and knotting it into a handkerchief, stashed it in her pocket. Yelena, in her hurry to get away before the woman could catch her watching, tripped on a root as she was stepping out of the lilac bush and wrenched her ankle. As she felt the ligaments stretch beyond their capacity, she crumpled to the ground with an involuntary whimper of pain. Immediately, the woman was at her side.

"Spying on me from behind the lilac?" she chided gently. "Is that what your mother taught you?" Clicking her tongue, the woman waited while Yelena examined her own ankle, and then helped her up. Balancing on her good foot, Yelena leaned heavily on the woman's shoulder.

"I'm sorry. Really, I didn't mean to be rude. It was just that your song was so beautiful, I couldn't help listening."

"Well, if you're going break your ankle spying, this is the place to do it. Saint Xenia is a powerful intercessor."

"I haven't broken it, just sprained it pretty badly," Yelena said, ruefully rubbing the injured area. "It'll be as swollen as an old *babushka's* tomorrow, and hurt like crazy; that, I can tell you for sure."

The woman bent to the earth again and dusted Yelena's burgeoning ankle with sandy loam from the chapel's foundation. Curiously unperturbed by what was obviously a superstitious gesture, Yelena looked down at the scarved head bent over her ankle, thoroughly enjoying the woman's motherly attentions. Just then, a flash of metal glinted in the evening sun and a small cross swung forward. The woman quickly put her hand to her neck and stowed it safely back under her blouse. Yelena asked her, almost sheepishly, "What's that song you were singing? I've never heard anything quite like it before."

"It's the *Akathist Hymn to the Mother of God*. Here now, lean on me and let's see if you can walk."

Yelena limped out onto the path with the small but surprisingly strong woman holding her by the waist. She bobbled a few steps and then stopped, looking into the woman's face. Her honest, tranquil blue eyes, such as were not often seen in Soviet society, where trust was a commodity you couldn't line up to buy, met her own squarely.

"I didn't know God was supposed to have had a mother," Yelena said. "Why is the song called an *Akathist*?"

"It's a Greek word that means it's not to be sung sitting. The hymn was written a very long time ago, when the city of Constantinople was saved from attack by the intervention of our *Bogoroditsa* – the Mother of God. We call her by that name because she gave birth to God as a mortal man: our Savior, Jesus Christ. The hymn thanks her for her interceding on our behalf, and praises her as the Queen of Heaven; it also names her the 'Unwedded Bride' because she became mother to the Son of God while miraculously remaining a virgin."

The surety and boldness of her answer shocked Yelena; the woman didn't seem to think what she was saying was in any way unbelievable. Yelena asked with incredulity coloring her voice, "Aren't you afraid to come here? It's as if you don't realize what you're doing. You should be more careful. How do you know I won't turn you in to the authorities?"

"I don't know that, dear," the woman said, smiling at Yelena's barrage of warnings. "Yes, they've closed our churches and hounded our priests into silence, but keeping believers from sharing the faith is like trying to dry up Lake Ladoga. It can't be done. If I'm shut up by the authorities, someone else will come to take my place. That's simply the way it is."

Yelena thanked the woman for her help and hobbled to the bus stop, barely making the last bus. Crawling into bed that night, she realized that in spite of their intimate encounter, she and the woman hadn't exchanged names. When she awoke the next morning, her ankle was as slim as ever and she felt not a smidgeon of pain.

CHAPTER VI

Leningrad, 1753

The night was windy and cold, and full of foreboding for Xenia. It was now the early hours of the morning, and although the troubled wife anxiously waited to hear her husband Andrei come through the door, all she heard was the howling wind outside the frosty windows. Normally, when Andrei was out, she didn't wait up for him, but this night felt like it was somehow different, and she could not fall asleep, despite her every effort. "I don't know why I'm waiting up for him; I'm sure all is well," she kept repeating, desperately trying to reassure herself.

She contemplated the events of the day to distract herself from the nagging sense of fear and uneasiness. She had enjoyed a lovely visit from her friends yesterday; they had discussed their favorite recipes for Lent, in which they fasted from meat and dairy, and had made plans for a festal outing in the spring. Yet no matter how much Xenia tried, sleep eluded her. She paced back and forth in the dark bedroom, glancing out the window, crossing herself over and over in silent prayer, desperately wanting to believe that Andrei was well and that there was a logical explanation for him not having returned home yet. She imagined that he would come through the door any minute, but her heart was not convinced.

During the past few years of marriage, Xenia had prayed continuously for a child. With her increasing prayer life, Divine Grace also blossomed in abundance, dampening the passion she once had for youthful partying and merry-making. Her dear desire now was that Andrei would stop his carousing too, or at the very least his overindulgent drinking, which by now had become habitual.

"Oh how I wish the Grand Duke and his friends would just leave my dear Andrei alone," Xenia often thought to herself with a sigh as she went about her daily housework. "While it is a blessing from God that Andrei was gifted with such a beautiful voice, it is also ironic that the same voice which gives his friends so much pleasure also seems to have turned into a curse for him. How I wish these people would realize what they're doing to him! Can't they see that he's drinking more and more each day that he is with them?" But then, as quickly as these thoughts crossed her mind, Xenia tried to subdue them, for she did not want to think ill of the future Emperor or of Andrei's comrades.

"I know that I shouldn't be thinking like this," she would silently whisper to God; "for it's a great blessing and honor that you have given Andrei the position that he has, and for that I give thanks." But even as she thought and prayed this, she realized that all the gossip and whisperings that had come to her attention over the years still plagued her mind.

Can what they say about the Empress Elizabeth and the court really be true? No, those things can't be possible; but why then does Andrei's greater contact with them weaken his character? Is it true that they are morally bankrupt? she asked herself. Xenia was terribly ashamed of herself for entertaining scandalous gossip about the Royal Family. She could not reconcile her faith in God's blessing upon her ruler with the evidence of human weakness unbefitting a Christian that continued to be discussed in all the social circles. Worry and sadness started to etch itself onto Xenia's face. When her friends stopped by for tea, it became more and more obvious that she was distressed about something, though she tried to hide it with her usual sweet smile.

"Xenia dear, you do not seem yourself," Tatiana said, putting down her cup of tea while looking soulfully into her friend's eyes during the visit yesterday.

"I am fine, Tatiana, it is nothing – just a little lack of sleep."

"A lack of sleep you say? What is doing this to you?" Tatiana asked inquisitively, while picking up one of the butter cookies Xenia had freshly baked that day in anticipation of their visit.

"Well, you know how much respect and admiration I have for the Royal Family, of course… " Xenia hesitated to finish her thought and started wiping up crumbs from the table while casting her eyes downward.

"Yes, of course, we all do, I don't understand why you are saying this, dearest one. What is troubling you about the Royal Family?" Tatiana pursued.

"Well… it's just that… well, they are taking up too much of Andrei's time, and I wish that they wouldn't, that's all!" Xenia burst out, quickly rising and walking to the cupboard, nervously fetching more cakes.

"Why Xenia, your intensity of feeling surprises me! What exactly is going on that has brought you to this point of upset?" Tatiana prodded with concern.

"Nothing, Tatiana, really it is nothing of note. I am just being silly. Please, tell me, how have you been feeling since the nasty cold you had a week ago? Your color is better, thanks be to God. Can I pour you another cup of hot tea?" Xenia deftly turned the conversation back to the concerns of her friends, typical of her truly selfless nature. Tatiana and the others knew not to prod further, and the conversation continued on more mundane topics.

Xenia regretted what she considered an outburst of her anxieties to her friends, and promised herself that she would not be so foolish as to voice them aloud again. She knew that the person she must talk with was her husband, and that until the right time came, she would pour out her heart to God and keep her worries to herself. However, despite her resolve, she felt increasingly resentful towards the Grand Duke and company each time Andrei came home wobbling on his feet, smelling of liquor and sleeping until noon. When he shook off the drunken stupor, he was generally the same charming and considerate husband, full of apologies for not being at home more often with her. Although she knew the rising problem must be addressed, Xenia never found an opportune moment to talk with Andrei soberly about the course of their lives. She wanted the good moments they had together to remain free of unpleasantness.

As her conscience began to weigh heavily on her with all of these thoughts and feelings, she desperately sought some kind of release. She decided that she would visit her spiritual father more often, and try to relieve her soul by confessing to him and partaking of the spiritual nectar he always offered as advice. She felt it had been too long since the last time she had done so.

Xenia left the window and returned to bed, determined to fall asleep with these pleasanter thoughts keeping her company.

Oh, it will be a joy to unburden myself in confession. Surely then I will have courage and the holy father will help me understand how to talk with Andrei, Xenia thought as she tossed and turned under the warm covers. The eerie howling of wolves far in the distance made her shudder involuntarily. She got up again after several minutes, wrapped herself in a robe to stave off the intense night cold, and went once again to look out the window. It was now the small hours of the morning, not long before the light would begin to emerge.

How strange to hear wolves outside the city tonight, she thought, remembering when she was a little girl, and an old *babushka* had told her mother that they had once been common in St. Petersburg, even entering the city and attacking people on occasion. This was, however, the first time that Xenia had ever heard wolves with her own ears.

She sat in a nearby armchair with a sigh, the sound of wolves' howls still echoing in her ears. But within minutes she was startled by a rumpus outside her house. There was a sharp clattering sound, which along with the strident neighing of a horse, seemed to shake the house.

"It's terrible how poorly this house is made," Xenia said aloud, frustrated, as she put on her slippers and went downstairs to see what was going on outside. "What a pity that our Tsar Peter built everything so hastily. Even the foundations are not as solid as they should be. Why just listen to this noise! Even the slightest movement on the street makes the windows rattle."

These thoughts, like buzzing flies, provided little distraction from the fear mounting into her throat. She felt the muscles tighten, and her heart beating faster as she descended the last steps. Even making the sign of the cross, which generally calmed her soul and body in difficult times, didn't quite shake off the intense anxiety and sense of foreboding she felt; it had troubled her all night, but was now approaching its apex as she reached for the doorknob.

"What is it?" shrilled a voice behind her before she could

open the door. Xenia's close friend, Paraskeva, who was like a sister to her and had been staying with Xenia for a month to keep her company, and who herself was also awakened by the noises on the street, came downstairs quickly to see what the commotion was about. "I heard the clamor outside, and began to get worried. Are you alright, my dear?" she asked anxiously.

"Oh Paraskeva, I believe that someone has stopped outside, in front of this very house. I am afraid that whoever it is will soon be coming to our door, and," her voice dropping to a whisper, "I dread the worst." Xenia's lip quivered as she let her eyes spill over, tears running down both cheeks.

"I cannot forget the terrible nights when I was told about my father's death," she continued, "and later, about my mother's death, too. It all seems to be happening again. Paraskeva, Paraskeva, please help me! I am scared!" Xenia grasped her friend's hand. "I am so scared that it will be bad news about Andrei because he has never come home this late!"

Paraskeva enveloped Xenia and held her tightly, distressed to see her friend in such a state of agony. Xenia began sobbing loudly. "I hope it's not bad news again; I don't know how I could bear it. I have such a terrible feeling."

"Shhh, hush, my dearest one...I am sure that Andrei is alright. You mustn't allow yourself to think the worst." Paraskeva tried reassuring Xenia as she continued hugging her and stroking her hair.

The knock that Xenia feared soon came. Someone was indeed at the door. Her legs began to weaken, and her head started spinning, but Paraskeva would not let go of her. She kept her tightly in her embrace, fearing that Xenia would not be able to stand without her help or even worse, that she might faint.

"Oh my dearest Xenia, please calm down, I am sure that it is nothing to fret about. We do have to open the door to see who it is, though," Paraskeva reasoned, reaching for the handle.

A sudden chill overtook them both as Paraskeva started to open the door, and neither could tell whether the chill was coming from the cold night air outside, or if it was something that came from within them. A royal servant posed in a deeply reverent bow before them. They instinctively knew that indeed, something was not right.

Paraskeva and Xenia both froze in fear upon seeing the servant, but quickly came back to their senses. The young man could not be left bowing at the door forever; he had to be addressed.

"What is it my dear man? Please, tell us what you are here for," Xenia, being the lady of the house, asked him softly, while gathering her strength and hoping against hope that her feelings of dread were mistaken.

The man straightened up, but he did it gradually and fearfully, for he was one of the Grand Duke Peter's servants, and knew full well the pain of a birch twig on his back, should he appear indolent and disrespectful. Not daring to look at either woman in the eyes, and mumbling in a low and humble voice, he said: "It's your husband, Colonel Andrei Theodorovich Petrov, my lady."

"My husband!" Xenia cried. "Speak up young man, speak up! What's wrong with my husband?"

"I am sorry, but he is dead," the servant answered.

"No! It is not possible, there must be some mistake," she said, as her body began trembling. "You see, he is at court, so he can't be dead," she explained to him, as if he were the one not comprehending the situation.

However, the look on the servant's face told her differently, and her worst fears of that fateful night had now become a grim reality. Xenia let out a cry of utter grief which desolately pierced the dark stillness and quiet of the early morning hours, eerily mingling with the distant howling of the wolves.

CHAPTER VII

Leningrad, 1963

Yelena had good news. Vanya and Irena, the couple who shared her apartment, were expecting a baby and had worked out a trade with a middle-aged couple in an effort to gain some extra room for their expanding family. The man and his wife had been sharing their three-room flat with their daughter and her new husband since the young pair had married six months ago. Last weekend the newlyweds were lucky enough to find more private quarters, so Vanya and Irena would take that family's three rooms, the parents would move into Sasha's cozy two-room flat, Sasha and Yelena would marry and he would move in with her. It was perfect. Of course, it could take months to work it all out with the housing authorities, but at least the end was in sight. She couldn't wait to tell him.

Yelena hadn't hear from Sasha since before her attempt to see him at the *Smolensk Cathedral*. Normally she would have been worried, but gaps in communication weren't unusual in their relationship because of Sasha's variable schedule and the fact that they lived at opposite ends of the city.

When she rang the phone on the bottom floor of his monstrous apartment building, the *dezhurnaya*⁺ who answered cut her off short, refusing to pass on a message to him. The old woman, who had the job of keeping an eye on the comings and goings of the building's residents, wasn't the lovable *babushka* type, but Yelena had never known her to be mean-spirited. Perplexed, she had no choice but to make the long trip across town to his workshop. When she got there, she found it empty once again. Now she was worried.

◆❚✽❚✽❚✽❚◆

At the hospital next morning, Yelena started her rounds with a troubled mind. She filed through the possibilities: he had injured himself at work; he had gone on holiday to someone's *dacha*[⌃] forgetting to tell her; or he was away working on a commissioned piece for an important person and couldn't contact her. None of the excuses she thought of seemed likely. But one plagued her: that Sasha had met someone else and he was avoiding her.

Evgenia appeared at her elbow just then with a stack of patient charts. She pointed to the empty bed where the Politburo member's daughter had been the day before.

"Vera went home."

"I know. I released her before I left last evening. I have to say I'm relieved she did so well. She's a sweet girl, but now we can stop making excuses for her to the other patients. Not to mention that the tension created by her mother's presence will disappear."

"Right," Evgenia said, nodding. Then she leaned in and whispered, "Do you know, before her parents came to get

---

⁺ A watchwoman, receptionist.

[⌃] A second home or vacation cottage.

her, that girl had distributed most of her toys and all of her candy around the ward to others. I had to go to each bed and gather them up after she had gone. Vera didn't get her disposition from that pinch-faced mother of hers, I can tell you that. She must have some relative at home making sure she learns her manners."

Having quickly diagnosed Vera with appendicitis, Yelena had performed the operation to remove the offending organ the morning after she was admitted. The girl recovered with remarkable speed. It wasn't really surprising, though, since getting the staff to use good hygiene was always the biggest obstacle to any patient's recovery. Several times, Yelena had observed the girl's mother bribing the staff to exchange her daughter's bed linens for fresh ones she'd brought from home, and twice she'd seen her coax an aide into applying a clean dressing by slipping a couple of three-ruble notes into the aide's apron pocket.

"By the way, Doctor," Evgenia said, "Nikolai's *babushka* is coming in to see you this morning. She's worried that he's not improving."

"I hate to say it," Yelena murmured, studying the boy's chart. "But I can't disagree with her. If only I could get some good antibiotics," she sighed wearily.

"You know that situation is hopeless right now," Evgenia said ruefully, shaking her head. Then her wide mouth split suddenly into a mischievous grin.

"Maybe you won't need antibiotics. Nikolai's grandmother has her own remedies, you know! After her last visit, I found dirt in a little bag under the boy's pillow," she chuckled. "With smart people like her still practicing that kind of superstition, how can we ever hope to make progress?" Rolling her bug-like eyes, she shrugged, still laughing, and turned away.

Yelena smiled, watching her sturdy ward matron walk

away, intrigued, as she often was, by the woman's gait. Evgenia had long spindly legs that seemed impossibly inadequate to support her heavy torso. She balanced on the toothpick appendages like a drunken acrobat, swaying to and fro for course correction as she made her way down the corridor.

It was nearly noon when an aide came to the door of the examination room that doubled as Yelena's office, to tell her that Nikolai's grandmother wished to see her. Yelena left her desk and went down the hall, stopping cold in her tracks as she entered the ward and saw who was sitting by Nikolai's bed. The woman looked up and smiled.

"So, we meet again." She rose and came over to Yelena who was still recovering her composure. "I am Marina Petrovna, Nikolai's grandmother. It appears as though your ankle wasn't sprained after all," she said with a knowing look.

Dirt under the pillow. Of course. Yelena thought to herself.

"No, it wasn't, evidently," Yelena responded, with a weak grin. "But don't let my incorrect diagnosis scare you. You can ask around, I have a pretty good reputation as a pediatrician." Yelena busied herself checking Nikolai's temperature and straightening his covers, trying to hide her discomfort. She was still trying to come up with an explanation for the strange incident. Her ankle had been decidedly sprained; there was no doubt in her mind. She could recall the exquisite pain and the initial swelling quite easily. Yet to have the sprain be completely healed the next day was wholly inexplicable; it should have taken days, weeks, to fully heal. The inconsistency of evidence and data had troubled Yelena greatly, but over the weeks she had dismissed it. Now, seeing the sweet-voiced elderly woman before her brought the whole uncomfortable situation rushing back to her mind.

Marina seated herself back on the bed next to Nikolai.

She had brought *borscht*⁺ with her in a fat glass jar and now poured some into a cup, holding it to her grandson's mouth.

"Please, *Babushka,* don't make me eat it," Nikolai said, turning his head.

Marina clucked, like a hen calling her chick to a worm.

"What are you talking about?" She brought the cup closer to Nikolai's mouth. "You love my *borscht.* Of course you'll eat, otherwise I'm going to leave this full jar for the doctor to take home with her."

"She can have it."

Yelena motioned Marina to come out to the hall. Marina put down the cup and Nikolai seemed grateful. She followed Yelena down the hall to her office. Once they were both in the room, Yelena shut the door. Marina's face registered alarm.

"What is it, Doctor? Is Niki dying?"

"No. No, Marina Petrovna. Nikolai is a very sick boy, but he's not going to die. Not if I have anything to do with it. Actually, I need to send him home. We have strict orders about patient turnover, but even putting that aside, there's really nothing we can do here that can't be done at home."

"Please explain; I don't understand," Marina said.

"Nikolai's been fighting off a bacterial infection, one that I am almost positive has left him with a chronic arthritic condition. The spiking fevers and the swollen, painful joints are classic symptoms. The worst of it is, if I'm correct in my diagnosis, and I believe I am, there is no cure. It would be good if I could give him antibiotics to clear any residual infection from his body, but antibiotics are out of supply at the moment and I don't know when we'll be receiving any. Perhaps you have a connection?"

⁺ A flavorful soup made with beets, giving it a characteristic dark red color.

Marina shook her head sadly.

"Then the best treatment we have for him right now is aspirin, and fortunately that is easy to come by. In the meantime I'll be seeing what I can do to get him into a rheumatology clinic, but as I'm sure you're aware, it may take some time. Not to mention the money you'll need to pass under the table in order to get a competent specialist. I'm sorry I can't give you better news, but this is the situation as I see it. I can make home visits to check on him, but that's the best I have to offer," Yelena explained.

"We're beating ourselves against the ice like fish the way it is," Marina said, shaking her head. "Since my daughter died – she was a doctor too, you know – and we lost her income, there's no extra cash for the kind of arrangement you're suggesting. I'm sorry, as we have been grateful for your care of Niki. God takes care of us though," she added, "and we don't grumble. Not too much, anyway."

"No, Marina Petrovna, you have misunderstood me," Yelena said quickly, peering at Nikolai's chart. "Your building's on my way home, I don't need payment to stop and check on my favorite patient."

She tried to seem nonchalant, as if seeing patients in their homes after hours for free was part of her daily routine. With Soviet medicine being what it was, surreptitious arrangements to circumvent the system were commonplace. Respected doctors like Yelena who had good reputations were often paid secretly in cash to visit Leningrad's more privileged citizens in their homes. The extra cash was nice, she didn't deny that. Especially when you considered the salary of any woman doctor was one-third that of her male counterpart. Someone would wink and hand you a patient chart into which had been slipped a few rubles and the promise of lots more if you'd only come to such and such address at such and such time. The practice had always splintered the heart of Yelena's principles, and even seemed a little sordid, but whenever she was summoned by important Party members to tend to their invariably spoiled offspring, she thought it best to comply. Visiting Nikolai at home would be a pleasure by comparison.

"No charge, Comrade," she said firmly. As soon as the commonplace address left her lips, Yelena saw Marina's expression flicker in an instant from relief to disdain, and realized that of course she was one of the elder generation who considered the now-proper title for all an affront.

Curiously, Yelena felt a twinge of guilt, rather than the usual irritation at this commonplace occurrence in her line of work. It made her realize that something in her did not want to disappoint this small, fiery, principled woman. "I mean, Marina Petrovna," she corrected herself.

Marina gave Yelena an appreciative look and rose, grasping the young doctor's face with both hands and warmly planting firm kisses on each cheek. Yelena's face felt hot and flushed as she showed Marina out the door. Under the confusion and perplexity she felt about this woman – such a collection of conundrums – she was actually quite pleased that she would be seeing her again.

◆▐✳▐✳▐✳▐◆

Riding the bus home later that evening, Yelena spied out the window the quieter old beggar she had bought a mug of *kvass* for months earlier. There were so many poor and bedraggled beings like him scattered throughout the city, despite the official high ideals of each citizen being well cared for. Yelena's heart felt as if it would burst with the sadness of it. And her firm resolve to do better, to work harder for those ideals, while yet carrying the weight of an unspoken futility she could not deny, felt like more than she could possibly bear. At times like this, she imagined turning her heart off like a switch, willing herself not to care so much, not to think or feel so much.

She wondered, with irony, whether he had prayed for his anonymous benefactress those months ago at the Church of Spilt Blood as he had said he would. She found herself imagining the scene: the wretched homeless man, unkempt and probably mentally ill, tottering pitifully down the street, falling to his knees upon the steps of the church, muttering meaningless prayers under his sour breath, for her. With a confused sigh, Yelena thought how very strange a scene it was to contemplate: foolishness and wisdom turned topsy-turvy, as if he were the one extending help to her, as if his empty words were more valuable than the coins with which she had pitied him.

Suddenly, the beggar outside turned toward the bus and caught her absentmindedly staring at him. Vivid green eyes seared hers for the span of a breath, sending goosebumps prickling up and down her arms. Time stood still as her breath frosted the window pane and the bus rumbled to life. Her gaze was riveted on that face – so curiously open and vulnerable, yet full of some warmth she could not comprehend. She felt as if, for that one moment, he could read her very thoughts. Blood rose to her cheeks, unbidden.

She noted the slightest unrecognizable gesture of his right hand, then turning on the foot of a crumpled, worn boot, he hobbled away without looking back. If there was such a thing as a soul, Yelena knew he had just examined hers the way a jeweler scrutinizes a gem, and found it to be of inferior quality.

CHAPTER VIII

Saint Petersburg, 1753

Andrei's funeral was held in the same Cathedral of Saints Peter and Paul that he and Xenia had been married in. The cathedral was an impressive structure, with a slim and elegant four-hundred-foot spire towering over the Imperial City. Donned in a somber black veil, Xenia recalled with a deep sigh that this same church was also the setting of the happiest day of her life. Today, however, the sweet memories of her wedding day made the pain of her grief even more acute. Hearing the deep solemn chants of the choir stung her with the realization of her husband's absence. "How often my Andrei chanted in this very church during the funerals of others," she thought, as the tears rolled down her cheeks, one quickly after the other.

The funeral service was an official affair, attended by the Empress Elizabeth, the Grand Duke and Duchess, and all the noblemen and women of the court. The Imperial Choristers chanted mournful hymns and lamentations for their fellow chorister with a fervor that was even more heartfelt than usual — for Andrei had been one of them.

Where are this world's pleasures?
Where is the display of glories that pass away?
Where are the gold and the silver?
Where are the throng of servants and their clamor?
All are ashes, dust, and shadows.
But come, let us cry to the immortal King:
"Judge him who has departed from us, O Lord, to be
worthy of Your eternal blessings.
Give rest to him in unending blessedness."⁺

All who were present on that sad day could not help but feel that special love, and to be deeply moved by it. Xenia and the mourners stood silently in their grief, as the ritual progressed and enveloped them into its ageless beauty and solemnity.

The rich sound of men's voices floated above them, mingling with sweet scents of incense, as these words struck deep chords in the listeners, deepest of all, perhaps, in Xenia. The reflective light of gold glittered from all sides, flickering in candlelight: the magnificent wall mosaics and gilded *iconostasis;*⁴ the shining objects of ritual: crosses, cups, banners and fans; the bishops in their richly-colored

---

⁺ From the Orthodox funeral service.

⁴ A wall connecting the nave, or body of the church, with the altar. It is often ornately carved or gilded and contains particular icons reflecting worship of God and important events in the life of Jesus, His Mother, and the early church.

robes and *omophoria*⁺ woven with golden threads, their miters and crosses that sparkled with diamonds, rubies and every precious stone. From every angle, sober faces shone: Christ, His beloved Mother, the Apostles and a myriad of saints looked upon the proceedings from their "windows to heaven,"ᐱ seeming to participate along with the mourners. In some, one might perceive compassion, in others, sobriety and detachedness, wisdom, or tenderness. What all the icons shared, however, was emanation of a pervading peace originating from beyond this world. All this was intended for the awakening of the senses towards the Almighty.

Although this was on a grander scale, all funerals in Imperial Russia were essentially the same. Having inherited the profound and other-worldly beauty of Old Byzantium centuries earlier,* Russia had taken this Christian faith and

---

⁺ A long strip of cloth draped around the shoulders; the distinguishing vestment of a bishop and the symbol of his spiritual and ecclesiastical authority.

ᐱ The term "windows to heaven" is used to describe Orthodox icons, which are created as a sacred space. More than just religious objects, they convey the presence of those depicted and provide a "window" through which those in this life can be present with those who have gone on before. The somber attitudes commonly depicted show the wisdom and grace attained through Christ and the subject's participation in the heavenly kingdom, beyond the temporal concerns of this world.

* In the year 988, Prince Vladimir had sent his emissaries throughout the Roman Empire, giving them the directive of choosing a religion for his people. When the emissaries attended the Church of the Haghia Sophia (Holy Wisdom) in Constantinople, they were overtaken by the celestial beauty of the surroundings, and together with the majesty of the Eastern Christian service, they found themselves in a state of wonderment and awe; for it was said that the grand church alone had three hundred chanters as well as walls of marble with shimmering mosaics of gold and precious stones. Upon their return to Kiev, the emissaries told the Prince about the splendor and how they didn't know "if they were in heaven or on

added to it a special grandeur that was uniquely its own. Through the funeral – its timeless ritual and inscrutable mysteries – the Orthodox Church ever offers its communicants the heights of ecstatic spirituality, extending consolation and hope to all who sorrow in the loss of a loved one, and recalling them to reflect upon their own lives, and to draw near to God.

When the lamentations came to a close, the Royal Choristers left the church in a deeply saddened state. They had not only lost a fellow singer in the person of Colonel Andrei Theodorovich Petrov, but also a close and beloved friend. The exuberance of his youth, his cheerful countenance, and the additional charisma of his excellent voice were all attributes that his friends would sorely miss. The shock of his sudden, unexpected and untimely death would surely leave an indelible mark on each and every one of them for the rest of their lives.

Xenia was filled with grief, for in addition to becoming a widow at the young age of twenty-six, and losing a husband whom she dearly loved, she was in the greatest distress that her husband had died without first confessing his sins. At the time of his sudden and unexpected death, Colonel Andrei Theodorovich Petrov did not have his full faculties. He was in a drunken state and was not able to either repent fully or to receive the holy sacraments.

"Oh my dear Lord, Jesus Christ," she cried silently to the heavens. "Please help my unfortunate husband, for he didn't mean to fall so far from Your Grace. I was also at fault and if only I had been able to give him a child, or had spoken out about my concerns, he might not have attended

---

earth." After listening to them, Prince Vladimir chose to adopt the Eastern Christian faith and go under the omophorion of the Patriarch of Constantinople. With this decision, he adopted the liturgy, worship and traditions of the Byzantine Church for his Russian people.

all those drunken parties." Yet no matter how much she prayed, her pain would not cease. For in addition to the unassuaged grief she felt over these things, Xenia was given an additional cause for suffering. During the entire forty days after the funeral, a period especially meaningful to Orthodox Christians as the soul makes its way heavenward, she would sense Andrei's presence, and he was seemingly pleading for her help: "Help me my dear Xenia, help me, pray for my wretched soul!"

As Andrei's desperate cries and pleas kept resounding in her heart, Xenia became increasingly distressed. Very little consoled her. Other than the love and concern of her dear friend Paraskeva, her only comfort was her uncle Theodore, who had also been Andrei's friend. Theodore was an officer and a nobleman in the same elite regiment as Andrei. His deep spiritual wisdom had often helped his cousins in their worries over the past years, and there was no one better for her to turn to in her time of need. She desperately required the comfort of his enlightened and consoling words, and they helped to keep her from despair.

Theodore, who would later become a monastic elder and future saint of the Church,[+] was also in deep mourning for his friend and comrade, for he, too, loved Andrei dearly, and he, too, heard his cries during the forty days that his soul traveled toward God. He knew well, as did Xenia, that when someone preoccupies himself solely with the secular delights of this temporal world and is ensnared by the pride which usually accompanies it, then the soul lacks the spiritual tenderness and humility which it needs to enter the Kingdom of Heaven. If one's heart at the time of his or her death is not in this condition, then it cannot absorb our

---

[+] Saint Theodore at first entered the Saints Alexander Nevsky Lavra and Sarov Monastery, but after suffering some distress, he became an elder with his own monastic order at the Sanaxar Monastery.

Lord's Love; only the recognition of our Lord's sovereignty and the humble acceptance of oneself as a sinner will prepare a person for union with God in His Kingdom. It was this very realization, in fact, precipitated by Andrei's untimely death, that made pious Theodore exchange the distinguished *Preobrazhensky Regiment* for the monastic life. He knew that belonging to the Regiment had been the main source of his, as well as his friend Andrei's, earthly pride. No doubt, his prayers through the ensuing years for his beloved niece Xenia were heard by God and would bear fruit past imagining.

◆❘✳❘✳❘✳❘◆

As for Xenia, her suffering had become almost unbearable. Though she would try, she could not get her husband's cries out of her mind. This agony confirmed to her the futility and vanity of the life they had led. "What good were the honors bestowed on him? They cannot do anything for him now," she would cry. Then, in a final act of desperation as well as one of charity and humility, she decided to give away all her possessions to the poor. This Christian gesture was not solely for her own soul, but even more so, as an act of charity for the benefit of the soul of her beloved Andrei.

She gave their beautiful house to her faithful friend who had remained by her side, the devout Paraskeva Antonova, with the stipulation that it would be a shelter for the homeless. Xenia hoped with her heart and soul that these acts of charity, mercy and sacrifice would serve as a kind of penance and help her husband receive the peace he so dearly wanted. As to be expected, these decisions were bound to cause trouble and scandal with Xenia's relatives who were not able to comprehend or fathom why she would do such a thing.

"Surely she must be insane," one of them said, with

intolerance written all over her face.

"No doubt," responded the other matter-of-factly.

Having convinced themselves of this, they went to the trustees of Xenia's estate in order to have them examine her sanity. Poor Xenia, suffering as she was in mourning and regret, had to endure this indignation as well. She was taken to court by her relatives and was examined and cross-examined. Of course, if she were to be found insane, then all her property would legally transfer to her greedy relatives.

"Xenia Grigorievna Petrov," asked the judge. "Why are you giving your possessions away? If you plan on pursuing a religious life and you have no need of them, then shouldn't your possessions be given to your relatives?"

"I believe that my relatives have enough to live on and that they do not need more," She answered meekly but honestly.

The judge continued with his line of questioning, until he had exhausted every possible angle. He decided that Xenia was indeed in her right mind, that she knew exactly what she was doing, and that her actions were both proper and correct for a pious Christian. He ruled the case in her favor, and together with the court, it was declared that she was even saner than those who had questioned her sanity! The case was thus closed, and Xenia Grigorievna, the wife of the late Colonel Andrei Theodorovich Petrov, was now free to do whatever she chose with her worldly goods.

"Most merciful Father," Xenia lamented as she prayed to the Lord. "I am such a sinner, and am filled with remorse. I should have been more forceful with my husband, and should not have concerned myself so much with the honor of his position and our own earthly wellbeing. What are those honors doing for him now? He is gone now, Heavenly Father, he is dead. I knew better and did not act. And thus, my Andrei left this earthly life without receiving the Holy

Mysteries, without the chance to repent and denounce his frivolous life. And for this I am in great distress for the sake of his soul.

"You took Andrei when he was intoxicated; how could he properly repent? Without denouncing his sins and being released from them, how could he open his heart to your love – the love which you give so willingly? He was not prepared to enter your Kingdom. Please help us, Heavenly Father, and relieve me of this terrible burden which my soul is now carrying. Please, in your great mercy and love for us sinners, tell me what I can do for him. In Your abundant mercy, there must be a way for him to reach Your salvation, to live with You in blessedness, for I know that You 'desire not the death of a sinner, but that he repent of the sins he has committed and live; and that even unto seventy times seven, his sins will be forgiven.'[+] What can I possibly do to relieve him of his earthly pride, when he's not on this earth anymore?"

Tears ran down Xenia's cheeks, as she lifted herself up from kneeling on the floor. She hoped for some enlightenment in answer to her heartfelt prayers and tears. Her hope sprung from the knowledge in her heart that God blesses those whose prayers are offered with love and humility, and that He loves, and forgives.

After the trial, Xenia Grigorievna realized that her ability to pray for the soul of Andrei was being hindered by her embittered relatives. The anger and animosity arising from their passions were disturbing her peace of mind, and she knew that quiet and peaceful contemplation at all costs was needed to appease her soul and help her husband. But she had difficulty eluding them. Her relatives considered her actions malicious, and with these suspicions, they also

---

[+] From the Orthodox prayer of absolution, which is said at Confession.

poisoned the minds of others. Everywhere Xenia went, false accusations were flung at her like barbs, disrupting her peace.

"Xenia, my dear, perhaps your mind is not working properly because of your distress. Let us go back to the judge and let him have a physician examine you," her aunt proposed to her.

"Xenia, how could you do this to yourself and to your family? You are a terrible person to abandon your family and to give your home to a perfect stranger rather than to those who are related to you!" her cousin snapped at her in passing one day at the market.

"Do you see that one over there, dressed in black? She is the contemptuous Xenia Grigorievna, who denied her relations any claim to her house out of spite," one woman whispered to her husband as Xenia was leaving the morning Liturgy.

The negative reactions that Saint Xenia received in passing, from acquaintances as well as from strangers, tormented her young and distressed soul greatly. Like countless saints before her and after her, the future Saint of God, Xenia, was unfairly gossiped about, slandered, and hounded.

Xenia, not having reached the spiritual maturity and heights that she would later attain through years of sacrifice, prayers and penance, was not yet strong enough to shun all secular concerns. She found herself in great mental anguish: spiritually oppressed and saddened by her relatives' slanderous remarks, and pressed upon to attend unendurable dignitary functions because of her station of nobility. Xenia decided to leave Saint Petersburg. She craved a place that would be more conducive to her spiritual life, a place where she could pray ceaselessly, without worldly distractions.

"Dear Blessed Mother of God, I must leave this place.

Please spread your mantle of protection around me as I embark on my own to find spiritual guidance," she prayed, making the sign of the cross upon her breast. She arose from her knees and kissed the icon of the Virgin Mary in her parish church, the same beautiful silver-encased image that she had prayed before and venerated so many times before throughout her young life. It was like an old friend to her, and she touched it gently with reverence and love.

Xenia Grigorievna left her beloved home and the sparkling city that held so many of her memories. She would not return or be seen again in St. Petersburg for eight long years. She told no one where she was going, but it was generally assumed she had joined a woman's monastery somewhere in order to pray for Andrei's anguished soul. Many also told the tale that after having lived a few years as a pious ascetic, she became a wanderer, and spent her time visiting the sacred sites of Russian pilgrimages.

CHAPTER IX

Leningrad, 1963

After standing for two hours in three different lines just to buy a little cheese, some sausage and a melon, Yelena was leaving the market with her string shopping bag less than half-full when she was jostled by a street sweeper. Caught off-guard, she teetered helplessly on the heel of one shoe. The street sweeper grabbed her by the shoulders, apologizing profusely while she found her balance. During the confusion, he pressed something into her hand, and as soon as she was composed he scurried across the street. Yelena recognized him. Sasha had once pointed the man out to her because he was a gifted painter who had been one of the Repyn Institute's brightest stars. She couldn't remember the details, but he had done something that had got him kicked out of the Union and demoted to his present lowly position. In any case, he was lucky to be working at all.

Yelena wondered, passing a corner trash barrel, whether or not she should dispose of the envelope the artist-turned-street-sweeper had put into her hand, but she didn't. As soon as she had boarded the bus and seated herself next to a snoozing *babushka*, she discreetly peeled back the paper the sausage was wrapped in, slid the envelope inside, and quickly retied the string around the package. But not before she saw her name written on the envelope in Sasha's hand.

By the time Yelena got off the bus a drizzling rain had started. Like any sensible Leningrader going about the city in full summer, she had an umbrella in her bag, but didn't bother putting it up for the half-block walk from the stop to her building. Feeling nearly sick with anticipation, she dashed past the *dezhurnaya* without a nod and headed up the four flights of stairs to her apartment. Her wet ponytail slapped against her neck as she bounded up.

Putting her key into the lock, she heard noises coming from the apartment. She groaned out loud. In the excitement, she had forgotten it was Vanya's and Irena's night off. They had visitors. The three couples were in the kitchen which served as Yelena's bedroom, cozied on the tiny sofa which was also Yelena's bed, drinking vodka and eating watermelon and sliced oranges. They were all talking at once, cackling like a flock of crows.

"Lena!" Vanya shouted, "Poor thing, you look like a drowned cat. Find a glass and join us. I'd get it for you, but my arms have gone numb." He flopped his arms like noodles while Irena, seated on his lap, collapsed onto his shoulder in a fit of giggles.

"Let me introduce you." Good-natured Vanya, his round nose red as a hot-house tomato, leaned forward woodenly, still pretending his arms were useless. Everyone in the group roared with laughter as he used his head in an exaggerated manner to point at each visitor in turn, "Nadia, Sergei, Mikhail, and Tatiana."

"Irena," Yelena said, ignoring Vanya's antics, "you should be careful with that vodka, it's not good for the baby."

With cotton-white hair and huge sapphire eyes, tiny Irena had a deceptively angelic appearance. She giggled, nestling into the crook of Vanya's arm, but her icy eyes glittered, warning Yelena to mind her own business.

Nodding quickly to the others, Yelena mumbled, "Nice to meet you all. Sorry. I'm not feeling well." She squeezed past the sofa, twisting deftly away from Mikhail's groping hand. Closing the bathroom door behind her, latching the flimsy hook-and-eye lock, she slid to the floor, leaned back against the wall with the string bag on her lap, and fished out the envelope which had become greasy and now smelled like sausage. Her heart pounded like a kettledrum in her ears. With trembling fingers, she took the creased and re-creased sheets of heavy yellow paper out of the envelope. Three pages covered in Sasha's tight, curving handwriting. After the first sentence, she read through tear-dimmed eyes.

Dearest Lena,

It is with great sorrow, and also with great joy that I write these lines to you. In sorrow, I'm afraid I must tell you that we will most likely never see one another again. In joy, I tell you that I have committed a crime of passion for which I'm incorrigibly unrepentant.

You're wondering, my angel, how this can be. I know your heart is beating like a captured bird behind your chest and your eyes are frightened to think what they might read, but please, I beg of you, hear me out, and then decide how you will think of me from now on.

It all started in the Smolensky Cemetery. No, that's not true. It began when my beloved babushka seized the opportunity during the religious thaw of '41 to have me baptized. I was seven years old, not a baby, so in a childish way I was aware of what was happening, and went away from the baptismal font knowing that I was somehow changed. I've told you, Lenetchka, that I am an orphan, that my parents died in an influenza epidemic and that my grandparents raised me. I must admit, however, that I haven't given you the whole truth. My mother was pregnant with me when my father Ivan, who was a priest, was arrested and sent to one of Stalin's labor camps where he only survived for one year. And I was only three months old when my mother, whose name was Galina, died of influenza.

My grandparents, Lev and Anna, were country people, pious and kind. They taught me about God, even took me to church during the war years when it wasn't so dangerous. But as I grew into a teenager, began to study art and became full of myself and my modern ideas, I saw their piety as simply cultural. I even came to pity them for their childish attachment to what I saw as provincial myths and fairy tales.

Always the liberal artist, you know, I never quite consented to the repression of our traditional Russian culture. I've often confused you, I think, with my diatribes against the senseless destruction of icons and churches. Until recently, the culture's religious expression was nothing more to me than a component of the whole. It was one manifestation of our creativity as a people, a product of the vivid Russian imagination, a vital part of our history that I thought should be preserved, not destroyed. But now I wonder if the real reason I felt so protective of our heritage was actually due to that seed of faith planted at my baptism. Being near the chapel and cemetery, hearing the hymns chanted, it has all stirred things within me these past months – made these issues more personal to me. Perhaps that seed, lying latent since my youth, has begun quietly germinating in the soil of my heart at long last. Like Pushkin's artist...

> But alien paints, in stride of years,
> Are falling down as a dust,
> The genius's masterpiece appears
> With former brilliance to us.

Like this, the darkly apparitions
Are leaving off my tortured heart,
And it again revives the visions
Of virgin days I left behind.

Within six months of each other, my grandparents died, leaving me entirely alone. I was only nineteen and they were the only family I had in the world, but I was a busy young artist feverishly dreaming of success and notoriety. I had no time for mourning. I've often heard that time plods like a tortoise when you're young and anxious for something to happen, but not so for me. The next four years marched by with the pace of a military parade. Next thing I knew I was celebrating my twenty-third birthday. I had just received my membership in the Union of Artists when you got on the bus at Nevsky Prospekt that day and took the seat next to me. Like magic, that city-clunker we were travelling in became an enchanted carriage for two. Do you remember, Lena, how we talked? You forgot to get off at your stop and so I stayed too. We rode and talked until the driver forced us off with threats!

But I'm straying. Back to the cemetery. Do you recall the singing, and how I complained about the old women who visited the grave of Blessed Xenia? (Yes. Take notice: I am calling her Blessed.) There was one woman who came particularly often. She came so often, in fact, that I became intrigued by her devotion as well as her lack of regard for her own safety, and so I began to watch her closely. She prayed with tears, often forcing small pieces of folded paper into the cracks in the walls of the chapel, and sometimes she would gather small handfuls of dirt from around the foundation and take them away in her pockets. Other visitors did that too, but she came most often. So, she was the one I kept an eye on, day after day. Once, after she had gone, I swiped the note she had just left in the wall and read it, and then I took out another and read it, too. Before I knew it I had read more than fifty notes.

Prayers. They were all prayers. All asking Blessed Xenia to please tell God this and ask Him that, as if the notoriously crazy old woman was an intimate and dear friend who had His ear. For the first time, I began to feel sorry that the chapel had been handed over to us sculptors for a studio. The prayers on those scraps of paper were so fervent and the faith of the believers who wrote them so strong, it seemed cruel that they couldn't go inside to say their prayers and worship their God.

One evening, just as I had put my tools away and was preparing to leave, I noticed a figure standing near the chapel. At first I thought it was the usual visitor, but drawing closer, I realized it couldn't be. The woman I'd been watching was short and always neatly dressed. This was a beggar. Tall, slender, and slightly stooped, she wore a tattered, pleated man's overcoat over a long dress and soft boots. A quilted peasant-style scarf covered her head. Turning to me she said in a formal, old-fashioned accent, "You're wasting precious time creating monuments to nothing. Stone towers crumble into dust, along with governments."

"Whatever you say, grandmother," I answered shortly, eager to be on my way. To tell the truth, I thought she must have had a bottle hidden somewhere under that moth-eaten coat and I didn't want to get involved, but what she said next stunned me into staying.

"You should use your skills to build something eternal," she said, sweeping her arm over the cemetery. "By repairing these crosses you can fix the commandment you've broken."

"And what commandment have I broken?" I asked, nonchalantly.

"The one that says you should honor your father and mother."

And with that she turned and sort of glided into the thickest stand of birch trees, disappearing from my sight. After she had gone, I went into the cemetery and walked among the ravaged graves for a long time. Writing them now, I realize the words the woman spoke were cryptic and strange, but you must realize that at the time they made perfect sense to me, striking my heart like well-aimed arrows. And when she mentioned the disrespect I had shown to my parents and grandparents, well, there she made a bull's-eye. By the time I left the cemetery, I had developed a strange, burning desire to do as she suggested, to repair the damage that had been done.

Once, I read a story about crates of oranges saving the lives of sailors suffering from rickets. Kruschev's generous policies toward cultural freedom were to us artists what those oranges were to the sailors in the story. The creative community was literally brought from the brink of death when he came to power. But just as we artists were enjoying unprecedented freedom, churches were being closed, outspoken priests arrested and believers harrassed. Lena, I know now what Kruschev doesn't, what I hope Russia will re-discover someday: true art and true religion are twins who share one heart. Creativity can't flourish where faith is suppressed. Every true artist, in the depths of his heart, longs to produce something eternal, something that will continue to inspire long after he is gone. But this is not possible so long as he refuses to acknowledge the origin of his gift. Once he makes that acclimation, he begins to produce something authentic. He stops lying through his hands and tells the truth.

Naturally, things being as they are, ᵢI was afraid as I contemplated my task, but apprehension was not stronger than my desire to right what was so wrong. Soon after, I began to work in secret, making excuses to stay late and working after dark, using discretion in my repairs so as not to make them too noticeable.   As I touched those crosses with my hands, honing and chiseling, cementing cracks and sanding them smooth, the damage our atheistic Soviet ideology had done to my soul began to be repaired as well. I began to believe again, as simply as if I were a child at my grandmother's knee. And I began to pray. Not long after, I struck up a conversation with

Marina, the small woman who comes to the chapel.

There is, I have discovered, a teeming world of believers hidden right in the open, visible only to those who have eyes to see: thousands like Marina, who are willing to risk their own safety in order to keep the faith. Complete strangers are closer than blood relatives. Through this invisible community a tiny New Testament not much bigger than a matchbook has come into my hands. For the first time I'm reading the words of Jesus Christ: "I am the resurrection and the life, he who believes in Me though he may die, he shall live." Because of the endless love Christ God has for the human race, He conquered death for us by dying voluntarily on a cross at the hands of human beings whom He had created. By His resurrection, he gave us immortality. You and I have believed in nothing, Lena. Atheism teaches us that death is simply the end. Looking at it that way, life is pointless. What are we here for? Are we ants? Living only for the material good of the colony and then dying off to make way for the next generation? No wonder you find your job of saving lives so depressing.

Lena, I am taking up my own cross. I am following Christ. I want to be counted as a fool for His sake. To step out on the narrow path, to walk the Way that ends in life. I don't know what the future holds, but I know that I no longer fear those who can kill the body; they hold no power over my soul.

I can't mention names of course, but it will be a believer who makes sure this letter reaches your hands. Risking your position and reputation is not my intention, my beloved Lena. Only, I couldn't be silent when I knew you were waiting and wondering. When you promised to marry me I was a very different man. You were proud of me then, I don't presume to hope you'll want me now. I'm releasing you from our engagement. Farewell. My love for you remains,

forever,

Sasha

With hot tears stinging her eyes, Yelena tore the letter into tiny bits and flushed them, a small handful at a time, down the toilet.

Sasha a Christian? Everything was changed now. All of the hours and hours they had dreamed together were gone with his letter. No more pretending, that was the truth of it. So many words and feelings they hadn't shared. So many secrets they had each been keeping. She was as guilty as he.

Like the night they saw that film about the American depression – what was it called? *The Grapes of Wrath*. They had stayed up nearly all night after viewing it, hashing over the evils of capitalism. The woes of the poor American people working for pennies, camping out like hobos, while the big businessmen lived in luxury, raking in the profits.

But even the pitiful people depicted in the film had been free to get in their truck, heaped with their possessions, and cross the continent in the possibility of a better life. That kind of thing didn't happen in Soviet Russia. And for all the gilt of the Soviet dream, there was a certain inescapable similarity between the ordinary citizen here and the migrant worker there. Party hotshots and government officials driving cars and shopping in exclusive markets for European luxuries while their compatriots languished on worn-out bus seats or waited in line to win a tube of vile toothpaste. She and Sasha hadn't discussed that obvious fact, though Yelena had mulled it over for hours after.

But Sasha a believer? How, exactly, did one go from being an intellectual atheist to an ignorant believer overnight? He'd explained it, hadn't he? A mysterious beggar woman. Crosses. Prayers. Believers. New Testaments. Jesus Christ. His Mother.... Love. Boundless love...

◆❘✳❘✳❘✳❘◆

When Yelena woke she was kneeling on the bathroom's ancient tiled floor, her nose inches from the mildewed grout. The gathering outside the door was growing rowdy. Someone was bound to need the bathroom soon. Briefly, she considered finding a glass as Vanya had suggested and joining the party. Instead, she grabbed her bag, and mumbling more excuses, threaded her way through the feet and legs crosshatching the narrow hallway between the sofa-bed and the wall. She stumbled down the stairs to the ground floor, used the telephone to call Nikolai's grandmother, and arranged to go over and see him.

CHAPTER X

St. Petersburg, 1762

The future Saint Xenia was born between two "Greats": two years after the death of Peter the Great, and two years before the birth of Catherine the Great. During her childhood and early adulthood, Xenia lived under the reign of the Empress Elizabeth, daughter of Peter the Great. After leaving Saint Petersburg on her eight year self-imposed exile, Xenia would return to the city shortly before the death of the Empress Elizabeth and the ensuing grand coronation of the new Empress, Catherine, which took place in Moscow. Catherine, however, would choose to rule the country from St. Petersburg.

Catherine, or *Figchen*[+] as her father affectionately called her, was to become a woman of great destiny. She was originally German, named Princess Sophie Auguste

---

[+] A German nickname meaning "little Frederica."

Frederike von Anhalt-Zerbst and she first arrived in Moscow in the year 1744 as the betrothed of the Grand Duke Peter,[+] nephew of the Empress Elizabeth, who was heir to the throne.

Catherine was bright and young and had all the proper credentials and qualifications for the wife of a future Russian Tsar, including an ancestry that could be traced back to the imperial Byzantine city of Constantinople. From the beginning of her life, fate was kind to Catherine, and everything she did worked to her favor. Besides all this, she also had the singular gift of making those around her love her. In fact; even the Russian people loved and embraced her as their Empress, despite the fact that she had not one drop of Russian blood! As their new Empress, Catherine willingly gave up her Lutheran faith, and sincerely embraced the Orthodox Church of Russia, while also mastering the language of her new country. The one thing which she was never able to do, however, despite her ability to speak fluent Russian, was to rid herself of the thick accent of her native German tongue.

◆|✳|◆|✳|◆

Before Catherine left Germany for her new life, her father, a devout Lutheran, begged her to not give up her Lutheran faith, because he felt that there were too many theological differences between Lutheranism and Orthodoxy. Despite this, Catherine arranged for her own consultation with Orthodox priests in her newly-adopted country, where she was advised differently. The priests told her that only the externals of the two faiths were different, but that the core belief was essentially the same. These

---

[+] Frederick II of Prussia, through his connections in the Russian imperial court, persuaded Elizabeth to decide in Catherine's favor as a wife suitable for the future tsar.

diplomatic comparisons satisfied Catherine so much that she was able to put aside her father's concerns without any guilt. In fact, Catherine's agreeable willingness to convert from her religion of birth would become a determining factor in establishing her future destiny.

Catherine, then a Grand Duchess, became a dedicated follower of her new faith and attended church regularly. This zeal for the Orthodox faith continued after she was married and became "Empress of the Russias." Catherine could be seen standing and worshipping for hours on end during the beautiful but lengthy Divine Liturgy. To the delight of all those around her, she never ceased to practice her new faith with piety and diligence. In time, all this became widely known and increasingly endeared Catherine to the Russian people, giving her an authenticity one could not manufacture or purchase. She became so loved by her subjects that she would come to be known and referred to as their "Little Mother."

When Empress Elizabeth died, the Grand Duke Peter was recognized as the *de facto* new Emperor, and Catherine, his imperial wife, despite not yet being officially crowned by the church. Tsar Peter III unfortunately did not outgrow the adolescent behavior that had wreaked havoc in Andrei's life through habitual carousing. His reputation for being obstinate, foolish and childish was widespread; and he excelled at creating ways of alienating his own Russian military. He required his guards to dress in Prussian⁺ uniforms and practice Prussian military routines for hours on end. He distinguished himself in an unflattering light by wearing only one decoration on his uniform: the Order of the Black Eagle of Prussia. Although his wife was German,

---

⁺ Prussia was previously a state in northern Europe. It became a military power in the 18th century and in 1871 led the formation of the German empire, which formally abolished it in 1947.

she was not Prussian; this strange devotion was inexplicable.

Tsar Peter's bizarre obsession with Prussia – its austerity and militarism – coupled with his idolization of its King, Frederick II, was considered an affront by his Russian subjects. They were humiliated by their ruler being in love with another country. His imposition of Prussian ideals had become especially insulting to his Royal Guards, which was a dangerous precedent. These elite guards, and especially the honorable and noble *Preobrazhensky Regiment*, of which Andrei had been a member, had previously fomented a devastating coup. Their activities had removed the child Emperor Ivan VI and placed Elizabeth on the throne instead. The Royal Guard was a powerful political entity and trying the patience of these venerated soldiers was extremely unwise for a ruler.

Peter made an additional error that would prove to be politically catastrophic for him. He openly showed his preference towards the Lutheran faith of his childhood, and upon becoming Emperor, one of his first acts was to construct a Lutheran chapel within the Royal Palace. He often attended services there, to the chagrin of his guards and attendants, as well as the Orthodox bishops and priests of Russia, who were soon to be officially crowning him Tsar through a sacred ceremony of the Orthodox Church.

Peter alienated himself still more by proclaiming an extreme decree: that all images were to be removed from Russian churches with the exception of those depicting our Lord Jesus Christ and the Mother of God. For the citizens of Russia, who had for centuries gazed upon and kissed icons of beloved hierarchs, saints, angels, and events of Christian history upon which their major feast days were built, this was a radical move, not to be borne without opposition.

When Peter publicized this fateful decree, he could make

claim to being Russia's secular head. But he was not yet coronated by the Orthodox Church, and could not make claim to being its spiritual head. "Spiritual Head" was a position and title decreed by his grandfather, Peter the Great, during his reign. Without this rightful anointing and title, his grandson Peter III did not have the right to make any decrees regarding the Church. This untenable situation made his position especially precarious, and Russia's loss of faith in her ruler was almost palpable on the streets of the major cities and forgotten byways.

Then to make matters even worse for himself, Peter heaped a barrage of insults and humiliations on his wife Catherine, who was immensely popular with the Royal Guards. This was due, no doubt, to Peter's own burning conscience, for the age-old story of desire and unfaithfulness was playing itself out again, this time at Catherine's expense. Peter announced his intention to divorce Catherine and marry his mistress, a woman from a powerful Russian family named Elizabeth Verontsova. She is known to have had only one distinction of note, and that was her lack of attributes.[+]

In these troubling circumstances, Catherine's friends and admirers, especially the Royal Guards over whom she held a considerable influence, feared that she would be imprisoned, assassinated, or at the very least sent to a monastery; so they acted on her behalf accordingly. Peter was quickly deposed in a coup by those loyal to his wife. Surprisingly, Catherine herself lead the charge on horseback, at the head of the *Preobrazhensky Regiment*.

[+] She was an unattractive woman with a tendency toward stooping, a physical liability that might have contributed to the contrived elegance in the bearing and carriage of Catherine the Great, something that her husband Peter would comment about disdainfully.

Catherine's name in Russian was Grand Duchess Ekaterina Alexievna. In order to please her subjects, Catherine had chosen not to use her father's German name as her middle name, though it is customary in Russia to do so. She was thirty-three years old when she took the throne, and she was to rule Russia as its Empress for thirty-three more years. With her husband Peter now deposed, Catherine began to make preparations for her own coronation in Moscow, the ancient capital of Russia, as soon as possible. She did not want to delay the Church's official blessing the way her husband had, for she knew that such a move would be much too dangerous, and she desperately wanted to feel that God was on her side. Catherine's reign would be one of benevolence and enlightenment in Russia and also one of greatness, for under her, Russia would become a world economic and military power.

◆❘✳❘✳❘✳❘◆

In order to raise Russia and its prestige on the world stage, Catherine knew that she had to make a grand show at her coronation. One of her first extravagances was to have a modern crown commissioned by the talents of a renowned Swiss jeweler. The crown consisted of five pounds of gold, five thousand diamonds, row upon row of precious pearls, and an enormous ruby topped with a diamond cross. This spectacular crown was to be divided into two distinct parts. One half would represent her as secular head of Russia, and the other as the spiritual head of the Church. When fully completed, it would weigh nine pounds in total!

"You know, Your Majesty," the jeweler said as he made preparations for the design, "the new crown might be too heavy for you to carry during the five-hour-long coronation ceremony."

Catherine, holding her head up high in her characteristic

way, and with a sparkle in her brilliant eyes, responded humorously to the jeweler's genuine concern.

"My dear man, are you not aware that in comparison to the new power that is now being given to me, the crown will feel as light as a feather?"

The jeweler chuckled politely, knowing that there was a great truth behind her casual remark.

The other regalia which Catherine had commissioned for the coronation were a scepter, which would later hold the famous Orlov diamond, and a round orb of solid gold. These would also be encrusted with diamonds as well as other precious jewels, and in order to have all this costly ornamentation made, the Imperial treasury had to be emptied of its largest and most valuable stones. A new carriage was also commissioned, completely gilded in gold, and a replica of the new imperial crown stood proudly on its top.

Tsaritsa Catherine's robe was resplendent in pure gold thread, and was embroidered with the double-headed eagle of Imperial Russia. Its lining was no less impressive: the fur of thousands of ermine. Finally, in order to please the crowds of Moscow who would crowd the streets to view this magnificent display, Catherine managed to collect over six-hundred-thousand silver rubles which she would generously toss to them the day after the ceremony.

The extravagant celebrations were to continue for an entire week, and they proved to be so lavish that the foreign dignitaries who were in attendance wrote letters home, saying that never before had they seen such prolific wealth and opulence. Catherine the Great's coronation defined a style of grandeur in Russian royalty that would continue until the godless Bolshevik revolution of 1917, and the martyrdom of Tsar Nicholas II.[+]

[+] The Bolshevik revolution was started by Lenin. He was sent by

Saint Xenia, much like the Empress Catherine, was also a woman of great destiny, but of an entirely different nature. For when our Saint Xenia reentered the city after an absence of eight years, she was not to enter it in a gilded carriage as Catherine did, but instead she entered it on foot, wearing ragged clothes and worn shoes without socks. Rather than multitudes gathered, cheering her into the city, Xenia's only chorus upon her arrival was a lonely birdsong.

The Great Catherine entered St. Petersburg wearing a golden crown bejeweled with the most precious stones. The crown our dear Xenia wore was even heavier than that of the Empress. It was not made of jewels and precious metal, nor was it made by the hand of man. Rather, Xenia's was a sacred crown given to her by our Lord Himself. A life of martyrdom was the blessed crown that Xenia herself had chosen, because of her love for our Lord.

Xenia's life was not one of earthly glories and vanities, but of unseen riches which are unimaginable for those without "eyes to see and ears to hear." She looked to a Kingdom far greater and more permanent than the one Catherine was given to rule. Xenia's Kingdom was one of eternal glory; with a crown that is given only to those who will meekly take their cross and follow Christ.

---

train from Germany into Russia in order to foment internal problems and hasten the defeat of Russia during the First World War. The sufferings brought on by the Revolution were not only felt by the Russian royal family and nobility, but by millions upon millions of others, including bishops and other clerics. It was during the revolution of 1917 that the reigning Tsar Nicholas, his wife and five children, as well as eleven of his Romanov relatives were murdered and martyred by the Bolsheviks. This ushered in an atheistic political system which tried to eliminate God from the people's consciousness. All of the martyred royals have since been canonized by the Russian Orthodox Church as Passion-bearers, with the exception of one Romanov, whose thoughts and actions were not conducive to sanctity.

While our great Empress Catherine was renowned for her collection of gowns – some made of priceless imported silks and damasks; some embroidered and trimmed with precious handmade lace; some shimmering with gold and silver; and others laden with priceless diamonds, rubies, emeralds and pearls, our Saint Xenia's gowns were only faded homespun and tattered rags.

As Empress Catherine warmed herself with jeweled ermines and sables throughout the mercilessly cold Russian winters, and huddled near warming fires that glowed and flickered in the stoves of her palatial homes, our poor dear Xenia would walk alone in the muddied and frozen streets with no stockings on her legs, and with only ragged and torn shoes on her frozen feet, willingly enduring the cold and accepting only meager offerings of food which the poor were able to spare for her.

While the great Empress had crowds cheering her everywhere she went, acclaiming her elegance and majesty in the streets, our dear Saint Xenia would be mocked and jeered at by any who saw her.

And while this great Catherine corresponded with rulers and gained accolades for her benevolence, enlightenment, and the knowledge she learned from Voltaire, Diderot, Grimm and the most brilliant and knowledgeable minds of Europe, our beloved Saint Xenia had no acclaim by the standards of this world. She was looked upon as nothing but a fool, a simple and insane fool, whenever she was even noticed at all.

And yet, both were women of great destiny; and the shared years of their lives was no mere coincidence, for God, through them, was now blessing Saint Petersburg and all of Russia both in this world and in the next. The great Empress Catherine II occupied the powerful throne of Russia and the Imperial seat of Saint Petersburg. A born leader known for her diplomatic and political astuteness, she was an enlightened Tsarina that in time would make Russia the greatest empire in the world. At the other extreme, on the dark, lonely streets of St. Petersburg's frigid *Petersburgskaya Storona*, a place that was plagued and distressed with every horror and tragedy imaginable, walked the blessed and humble Saint Xenia, a woman of great faith and sacrifice. She was placed there by God Himself in order to pray for, and to oversee, the spiritual welfare of His people.

CHAPTER XI

Leningrad, 1963

If Yelena's apartment building typified the grace of old St. Petersburg, Marina's was the epitome of modern Leningrad. Hulking, stark, and pitted by regiments of concrete balconies, it loomed over the sidewalk in a state of premature aging.

When Yelena approached the double glass doors leading into the lobby, Marina stepped out of the shadows and took her by the arm. Peering around the door, she gave Yelena a pointed look and they eased past the heavy-eyed *babushka* security guard and up the stairs to Marina's flat. Marina unlocked the door with her key, calling out in a sing-song voice, "Niki, look who's come to see you!"

Nikolai was sitting on a sofa which, like Yelena's, appeared to do double duty as a bed. He waved the toy truck he held in his hand. "*Privyet*, Doctor. I don't have to go back to the hospital, do I?"

"No," Yelena smiled. "You're fine where you are. I was just passing by and thought to myself, 'I wonder how my favorite patient is feeling today?' So I came on up to see for myself. And I must say, you do look well."

After a brief examination, Yelena ruffled Nikolai's blond hair and dropped a kiss on top of his head. Marina motioned Yelena over to the kitchen table where she was pouring tea into glass cups cradled in tarnished gold-plated holders. She had already sliced a loaf of black bread and some cheese and arranged it on a plate.

"Sit, sit, sit, my dear," she commanded, and Yelena did.

"Marina Petrovna, why didn't you tell me on the telephone that Nikolai was so much better, and that he has gone into remission? I can hardly believe my eyes. I've never seen a case of arthritic inflammation resolve this quickly!" Yelena remarked, picking up her cup. The tea was strong, sweet, and very hot, just the way she and any other self-respecting Russian liked it.

"I was afraid you wouldn't come otherwise, my dear. And besides, I wanted you to see for yourself. It's another miracle, worked through the prayers of Blessed Xenia," Marina explained.

Was the woman incurably deluded? Yelena had been going to launch into an explanation of how remissions in rheumatic arthritic conditions occur, but Marina's answer silenced her, as she didn't want to offend her hostess. No one really knew a definitive process from science, anyway; their theories were little more than "best guesses" or observations without explanations. Perhaps Marina's answer was just as reliable. And then there was still the strange matter of her ankle that couldn't be explained...

Yelena shook the thought away. "Do you and Nikolai have this flat all to yourselves?"

"My son-in-law Dmitri lived here with us until recently," Marina said, and then added in a whisper, "He re-married about a month ago. His new wife is young and doesn't want to raise another woman's child. Dmitri is a good man, he's still supporting us, but Nikolai will stay here with me."

"Please tell me about Blessed Xenia, Marina Petrovna," Yelena burst out suddenly, to her own surprise. "I want to know her story."

Marina's gaze was long and keen. "And you want to know what made Sasha do what he did," she said, her gentle almond-shaped eyes full of understanding. "I wondered when we would get around to it. Well, I'll tell you all I know about Saint Xenia, but about Sasha I can only tell you that the ways of God are beyond our comprehension. It was He who made us, not the other way around. You and I may be able to hide the secrets of our hearts from each other but we can hide nothing from the One who sees everything. God saw something in Sasha that you had missed, apparently."

"No. I didn't miss it," Yelena said, shaking her head. "I think somewhere, deep down, I knew something was changing in him. And he has always been different from other men, quoting Pushkin and reading smuggled copies of Gogol and Dostoevsky. He feels things so deeply, things no one else seems to care about."

"I'd venture to guess it was that difference that attracted you to him in the first place," Marina said, refilling Yelena's cup and putting another bit of cheese on her plate.

"Maybe you're right." Yelena took a bite of cheese and sipped her tea, pondering that possibility. "I'm beginning to wonder if we weren't both hiding from ourselves, and each other, these last months. Ever since I first visited Sasha at his workshop and heard you and the others singing, I've been haunted by memories myself."

Marina crossed the room to lay a thin, tattered quilt over Nikolai, who had fallen asleep. Watching her, Yelena was reminded of the tiny songbirds that came to Leningrad's parks in the early summertime, flitting about, making their nests and feeding their young. Marina came back to sit, catching Yelena's eye with a keen look.

"What kind of memories?"

"Memories of my childhood," she answered directly. "Sasha and I were both orphans, you know. That was one of the first things we discovered we had in common. My parents were both casualties of the siege shortly after I was born. They're buried with the thousands in the *Piskarevskoye Cemetery*. As an infant, I lived briefly with my aunt and uncle, but they gave me up to a woman who lived on the outskirts of the city in order to save me from starvation, a fate they both succumbed to later."

Marina nodded. Everyone in Leningrad had a siege-story, or knew someone who had one to tell. "Was the woman good to you? They weren't all kind, you know. The people who took in orphans during the war."

"Oh, yes. She was very good to me. Her name was Mariya. She had just lost a baby boy to pneumonia – so recently, that her milk hadn't gone dry yet. I'm told she nursed me in his place, though she must have been grieving terribly. She was very kind. A sweet-tempered woman. And a believer. That's what I'm getting at, Marina Petrovna. Lately, I've been having these snatches of memories and images – sometimes not just images, but sounds and smells too, will suddenly overpower me. Church bells ringing, priests censing. A splash of color and a penetrating face flickering in candlelight. But there is one memory that's plaguing me most of all."

Marina leaned forward, gently taking her hand. "Tell it to me."

"We are all inside the church. I'm hiding in Mama's skirts. I liked to do that. Sometimes I would even duck inside them (they were so full) and hold my own little private service. Of course Mama would make me come out, but this time I was just wrapped in the outside edges looking around, listening to the chanting, half-daydreaming, when a group of men suddenly stormed into the church screaming at everyone and shoving the worshipers outside. Some of the *babushkas* and *dedushkas*[+] were still in the middle of a bow, their arms forming the sign of the cross while they were being dragged out the door. Soon the men had forced everyone except the priest outside and while Mama held me in her arms, we watched the church go up in flames, columns of smoke billowing like satanic cupolas up to the sky. To my child's mind, the crackling of the fire was heaven crying out in pain.

"Even though the priest was old and feeble he had tried to stop them entering the holy of holies,[⌃] but they knocked him down and torched the altar first. One of the grandfathers went back into the church and pulled the priest out. He lay on the ground choking from inhaled smoke. His robes and beard were burnt; we could smell his singed hair – it was horrible. Then the men climbed up on the roof and cut the bells down, pitching them to the ground just before the fire reached the bell tower. As soon as they were sure the church was beyond saving, the men went away as fast as they had come.

"With tears in their eyes, Mama and the other women began to sing hymns. They sang all night, holding vigil until the church was just a smoking heap of rubble and it was too cold to linger. One of the hymns I remember well. It was the same one you were singing in the cemetery that day. I lied when I said I'd never heard it before, and also when I pretended that I didn't know about the Mother of God. I'll never forget those words, we clung to them like a rock in a storm: *Rejoice, Unwedded Bride.*"

Yelena put her head on her arms and her shoulders

[+] Grandfathers, elderly men.

[⌃] Inner chamber of the Orthodox church where the altar and precious vessels reside. Only ordained clergy are allowed to enter.

shook with sobs as the relief of having finally given voice to the thing she had suppressed for so long coursed through her. Marina waited, letting her cry it out. Then she said, "Where is your foster mother now?"

"She died in an influenza epidemic. That's another thing Sasha and I have in common. We are both completely alone in the world. Oh, Marishka," Yelena cried pitifully, unconsciously using the tender nickname, "what am I going to do without him? I don't even know where he is!"

Marina took Yelena into her arms, stroking her hair. It felt good to cry. When Yelena had calmed a little, Marina held her at arms length, looking intently into her eyes.

"Yelena, listen carefully. I know where Sasha is. And I know something else, too. That he loves you. More than ever, but not more than he loves God. You have a choice to make. Do you choose to live as you are, a respected Soviet doctor and atheist, without Sasha? Or do you choose Christ, as I believe you've already done in your heart of hearts – whether you realize it or not – and go to be the wife of a dissident Christian artist living in exile? Will you love and cherish a "parasite on society" - an enemy of the State? And become the same yourself? It's all up to you."

Marina paused a moment, letting her words sink in, then pushed away from the table and began carrying cups to the sink.

"You'd better stay the night and sleep on it," she said. "It's too late for you to go home now. And besides, I haven't told you about Blessed Xenia."

◆❘✳❘✳❘✳❘◆

Yelena woke early to find Marina's side of the bed already empty. She was standing in front of the sink when Yelena came into the kitchen. Having pulled aside a decorative curtain to reveal a trio of icons, she was praying in a low voice. Yelena stood just behind her, basking in the warmth of the older woman's well-worn prayer, and when Marina made the sign of the cross to finish, Yelena followed suit, pressing her fingers and thumb against her forehead in the way that her foster mother had taught her long ago.

"It won't be an easy life, you know," Marina said, without turning around.

Yelena wrapped her arms around the little woman from behind, resting her chin on Marina's head. "I know," she said, softly.

CHAPTER XII

St. Petersburg, 1761

During her eight long years of exile and absence from St. Petersburg, Xenia would pray on her knees each day with tears and humility:

"Dear Lord, I cannot get Andrei's cries out of my mind. I don't know what to do; but I know that you are always so merciful to us. Andrei is not in this world anymore, and therefore he is not able to repent for his sins. He has removed himself somewhere distant and far from your love, but I am still here and still have the time to repent. In your mercy, I know there is a way. Love is eternal, and patient and kind; I know that the love I have can somehow be offered as a sacrifice for my husband, if it is done in Your Love. Please show me a way.

"What if I were to offer myself in humility as a replacement for Andrei? What if, dear Heavenly Father, I was to stand before you in his name, and substitute myself for him? Then it would be as if he was still in this world in the "person" of myself. Surely, then, you would have to hear his cries, and open your ears to his penances, the penances that I will be doing in his name. If it is all done for love's sake and in true humility, surely it will be for my salvation as well as his, and You will hear us, and answer in faithfulness."

Xenia would visit monastery after monastery, praying endlessly to God for direction, and benefitting from the spiritual counsel of holy monastics, who encouraged her course. In so doing, Xenia grew in God's grace exceedingly, beginning to emulate in action and countenance the saints of old.

In the spiritual journey of those who are very pious, one recognizes in his soul when God has enlightened him to embark upon a particular path. It was exactly in this manner that Xenia knew that she should finally return to St. Petersburg. Xenia was now immersed so completely in the grace of God, that she knew exactly and without a doubt how she had to proceed, and what God's will for her was.

Upon returning to Saint Petersburg, Xenia went to the impressive home she had given to her friend Paraskeva Antonova, knocking meekly on the door. When Paraskeva opened the door, she did not even recognize her former friend and benefactress. She simply saw a worn woman before her with old, ragged clothes, and assumed it was one of the many beggars she saw in the streets, now seeking alms and shelter at a residence where she had good hope of receiving it.

"Come in, my dear person," she said compassionately, with unfeigned warmth.

"Paraskeva, my dear Paraskeva, how are you, my beloved friend?" Xenia responded with feeling, as she moved forward her to hug her.

Paraskeva Antonova instinctively stepped back because of the unease she felt at such familiarity from someone she didn't know. But within a split second, she also recognized that there was something familiar about this voice. After pausing a moment as realization dawned, she asked cautiously, "Can it be you, my dear Xenia?"

"Yes, it is me – It is Xenia!" The woman in layers and a peasant kerchief knotted under her chin nodded with a sweet and unmistakable smile.

Without any further words or hesitation, Paraskeva enveloped her beloved friend in a long and warm embrace, and then fervently kissed her the customary three times. She hugged Xenia closely, as if she never wanted to let her go.

"Oh Xenia my dear, you look so worn and tired," Paraskeva said, as her eyes started watering. "Do you have any idea how much I have missed you, how much I have prayed for you and wondered about you?

"Here, my dear one, sit down as I make some tea in the samovar. You will see how much better you will feel, and then you can tell me all about your experiences. But first, please tell me, where were you all these years?" She sat beside her old friend and looked into her eyes, while taking Xenia's hand into her own.

"I had worried and worried about you over many sleepless nights," she continued, "but as the years went by, I feared that perhaps I had lost you forever; though I confess that I never stopped hoping that God would grant me the blessing to see you again."

Paraskeva's voice cracked as she wiped away a stray tear with her fingers, whispering, "I missed you so much." The tears began rolling unbidden down her cheeks, and she quickly grabbed the corner of her apron to wipe them away.

Xenia looked closely at Paraskeva, and seeing the deep love reflected in her eyes, was overtaken with compassion for her old friend. She had missed this rare bond of friendship and familiarity in her sad, prayerful, and often lonely pilgrimage.

"Oh my beloved friend, I will only be able to stay with you for a short while, and that much I will do only because I love you so very much. I have been given a precious gift in my years of sojourn, and I must remain in continuous and steadfast prayer, without being deterred, even by the sweetness of a dear spiritual sister. My beloved Andrei is still not at peace and I must retrieve his uniform."

"Yes, I will get it for you, and whatever else you want. They are yours, of course; I have only been steward of it all in your absence," Paraskeva said with sincerity. Destitute of an inheritance or livelihood, she had always been totally dependent upon the charity and kindness of Xenia and her parents.

Paraskeva Antonova and Xenia Grigorievna had been close friends since their childhood. Paraskeva lost her family at a young age, and she was taken in by Xenia's parents to be loved and cared for, and to be a sister to their daughter, who was so often alone. Paraskeva was treated with Christian kindness by Xenia and her family. They gave her all the love that her young soul required and thirsted for, as well as a solid and devout Orthodox Christian upbringing.

Paraskeva was extremely grateful to Xenia for giving the house to her before leaving Saint Petersburg. It gave her some means to support herself, as well as resources to help the beggars who came to the door for alms and shelter. Paraskeva Antonova worked long hours each day, producing the handiwork which had become her specialty. She became a renowned seamstress, and her embroidery was coveted by wealthy patrons for its excellence. Her fine hand also produced a lace that was so exquisite and delicate that it was praised throughout Saint Petersburg, and was even sought out by wealthy patrons as far away as Moscow.

Paraskeva Antonova found that through her talent and

hard work, she was able to provide for herself quite well, and for that, she never stopped thanking God for His goodness. Paraskeva had few personal needs, and rather than save extra money for the day when she would not be able to provide for herself, she did what the holy and blessed Xenia wanted her to do. She fed and helped the poor and destitute that came to her door.

Acquaintances and friends wondered what would happen to Paraskeva in her later years when her eyes would fail her and she would not be able to make her delicate treasures. For Paraskeva Antonova though, there was only one answer to their worries, and that was to put all her faith in God, the Father of all, the Keeper of the sparrow.

That faith, though foolish to the minds of unbelievers, would not fail Paraskeva, for shortly after their reunion, Xenia re-entered the house abruptly and said in an unusually urgent manner, "Here you are sewing, and you don't even realize that God has given you a son!"

"A son? What are talking about, my dear Xenia? I am not even married!" Paraskeva exclaimed, looking truly confused and perplexed at her friend's strange outburst.

"Go at once!" Xenia replied urgently. "Quickly, quickly, you must go to the *Smolensk Cemetery* – You must go NOW!" Xenia insisted with authority.

For one second Paraskeva hesitated, but then remembering that her pious and saintly friend would never say anything idly, she complied. She quickly grabbed a warm shawl to wrap herself in, and she hurriedly ran out of the house to get to the *Smolensk Cemetery* with all speed.

"Xenia must know something, to be acting this way," she reassured herself, walking quickly towards the cemetery. As she crossed a street, she noticed a large gathering of people looking at something. She asked one of the gentlemen in the crowd what all the commotion was about, and was told that there had been a serious accident.

Upon hearing this, she ran quickly to assist them. "Please, please, let me through," she begged the people in the crowd, as she pushed them gently aside. "I want to be of help!" she cried.

When she reached the front of the crowd, she noticed a very pregnant woman lying on the ground in a large pool of blood. A coach had accidentally knocked her down, and the distraught coachman was beside himself, not knowing what to do. The woman was moaning with pain, and began giving birth to her child. Despite the unusual circumstances, the baby came into life healthy and crying, though the unfortunate woman was in painful agony from the trauma of the accident.

Without hesitation, Paraskeva Antonova took off her shawl and reached down for the child, whom a compassionate bystander had helped to deliver. Paraskeva deftly wrapped the newborn baby in it for warmth. She then cried out to the crowd, "Someone please – quickly call for a priest! This woman is dying and she must be given the sacraments!"

Handing the baby to the coachman, she held the woman's head in her arms and began singing hymns. "Please pray with me," she said kindly and tenderly to her, and as the woman began praying, her pains began to subside. She was able to gather enough strength to ask Paraskeva about her child, and Paraskeva let the unfortunate woman know that it was a baby boy and that he was healthy and well; and she reassured the dying mother that he would be well taken care of.

"By whom?" the mother whispered with concern, her strength quickly waning.

"If no one else, by me, myself," promised Paraskeva, realizing with awe the power of Xenia's prophecy to her only moments before.

Shortly after, a priest arrived and knelt beside the

woman. "Here, here, my dear," he said, as he brought his ear down to her mouth so that he could hear her confession, gratefully given. Immediately after, he administered Holy Unction and helped her take Holy Communion. A moment after swallowing, the woman breathed her last, for it seems our Lord, in His love and mercy, kept her alive until she could partake of the blessed sacraments. The poor young mother could not have been more than seventeen years old when she died.

Paraskeva immediately felt a deep compassion for the newborn infant who was now motherless. She bundled him close to her own shivering body, and hurried home with him, stopping only to call at her neighbor's house to bid her to find a wet nurse with all haste, for the orphaned infant would soon be hungry. Once inside, she carefully unwrapped him near the warmth hearth and wiped his tiny face and perfect little body clean and dry before swaddling him in soft linen. His eyes were wide and blue, searching the depths of her own with wonder. He gazed at her with complete trust, and Paraskeva knew peace as she had never known it before.

Later in the evening, police officers came to Paraskeva's house. "Please, officers, I entreat you to find the father, or at least some other relative of this infant," she begged them, both respectfully and adamantly. She felt that whoever the family might be, they would be devastated to learn what had happened to the poor woman and frantic to locate her child.

"We'll try as best we can," one officer replied, wanting to be as helpful as possible, for her sake as well as the child's. Local authorities all had the greatest respect for Paraskeva and the abundant charity she tirelessly offered to those in greatest need of help, whom the government had largely forgotten.

A few days later, the same officer returned with sad

news. "I'm sorry, my dear Mistress Antonova, but we have looked and asked tirelessly for the whereabouts of some relative. No one in Saint Petersburg is willing to claim either the child or the mother. Through all channels of communication, there has been no response at all. We can only assume that the baby is illegitimate, and that the father and the parents of the girl do not want to make claim of the child for fear of a scandal. She was awfully young, you know. I'm afraid he is officially an orphan."

Knowing that the poor dead woman was unrecognized and would only be given the poorest of burials, Paraskeva provided a funeral for her. If nothing else, at least she could comfort the mother's soul with her prayers and the presence of her son at the service, where no one else but a lone chanter and gentle-voiced priest attended. Paraskeva decided to keep the poor orphaned infant as her own, fulfilling both her promise and her heart's desire.

"Oh my sweet little precious one, don't you fret," Paraskeva whispered to the infant as she rocked him in her arms, walking back and forth to quiet his tears. "I am here, and I promise you that I will love you and will provide all that you need," and at that promise, as if understanding her language of love, the infant stopped crying and fell asleep in her reassuring arms.

Indeed, Paraskeva went on to raise the orphaned baby boy, providing him with motherly love, a healthy and devout upbringing, and a good education. Years later, this boy whom she loved so dearly, grew up to be a fine young man and became established in his own right. He was then able to take care of his beloved foster mother, the woman to whom he owed his blessed life, in her old age.

+ *Our Lord Provides.* +

CHAPTER XIII

Leningrad, 1963

A week later, after their morning prayers, Marina motioned for Yelena to sit at the small square table pushed against one wall of the kitchen. Like everything else about the home, it was old and well-worn, but scrubbed clean. Yelena gently traced a bright red poppy embroidered on the centerpiece, admiring the fine border of precisely-interlocking squares and diamonds along its edge. Although her hands were skilled in other ways, she could never understand how some women could so patiently create these objects of beauty with a needle and thread. They were such simple, overlooked arts, but they made a home cheerful and full of life, rather than drab and utilitarian.

Marina placed a hot plate before her with two perfectly poached eggs crowned atop a thick buttered slice of dark toast. A cup of stout black coffee steamed beside it. Yelena exclaimed in surprise: "Coffee! Wherever did you get it? And two eggs – so extravagant! With butter, no less! Are you sure you have enough for yourselves? I can easily get by with one. Here, Marishka, let me share with you."

"No, no, my dear. You eat. You have a long day of work ahead of you as well as important things to contemplate. Niki and I have plenty," she insisted.

A thin voiced piped from the living room: "Baba, I have finished my prayer rope.⁺ What's for breakfast?"

"A treat, my dove! The last of the gooseberry jam we made on toast."

Niki chuckled in delight and Marina smiled indulgently at the sound, sighing, "I've missed that exuberance. Thanks to the prayers of Blessed Xenia it has finally returned. And rightly so, for today is a day of celebration for all of us, for you have started on the path to salvation." Her warm smile embraced Yelena as she spread the sticky dark red jam and brought it out to Niki with a large glass of milk.

Then, sitting with her toast and tea, Marina looked pointedly at Yelena, as if sizing her up. "You understand that these days it is becoming dangerous again to be openly religious, especially for young people such as yourself with great hopes for Soviet glory and productivity."

"Yes, of course," said Yelena matter-of-factly, the decadent coffee filling her senses as she sipped.

"It is one thing to be an old harmless *babushka* full of foolish superstitions, but quite another to be a young model Communist ideologue who 'defects' or 'becomes a traitor' to the state – especially, in your case, one educated as a brilliant physician at the state's expense who has ardently supported the party line. To lose an earnest idealist is a big blow."

Yelena was shocked by Marina's frankness. As she took in the phrase "model Communist ideologue" and saw, as it were, herself – her old self – in a new light, she realized that

---

⁺ A necklace or bracelet made of knotted wool or silk. At each knot the small prayer is recited: *Lord Jesus Christ, Son of God, have mercy on me (a sinner)* – sometimes referred to as the "prayer of the heart."

this unimposing old woman was anything but ignorant. She was smart as a whip, and comprehended much more than she let on. The ensuing conversation revealed to Yelena the complexity of that network of Christians Sasha had alluded to in his letter and the lengths they went to in continuing their hidden life of piety and in protecting one another. She was amazed that so much could be happening all around her without her knowledge – and that so many more people could be numbered among the faithful than she had ever imagined. The whole thing was a bit humbling.

Even in her humility, as she listened, Yelena's heart felt free after years of imprisonment. She felt a beauty being unlocked there, opening like a bright red poppy, after years of pounding upon it with the drab, utilitarian ideals she had forced herself to embrace. Once considered all-important, those ideals now fell away, empty and lifeless. Yelena looked squarely at the unfulfilled promises of communism she had tried to wish away for so long, and recognized them as the empty lies they truly were.

In their place, this dawning beauty was at the core of her heart. She had known it from a child, known it all along. Like an ember, it had remained, glowing, even though it had seemed extinguished. The fact that faith and belief could be this resilient in herself and in the Russian people, could be this alive and powerful despite the imprisonments, the martyrdoms, the intellectual barrages upon the collective psyche, was so full of hope it brought tears to her eyes. Here was the True Ideal. Here it was in a Person, One who called forth the best of ideals – love, forgiveness, hope, beauty, truth, and joy – in His followers. Through Marina's explanations she could suddenly see it all, and that it had always been there, only obscured from her view.

Glancing at the clock, Yelena gasped in surprise. "I must go immediately! I knew I was going to be late, but not this late!" It felt as though she was tearing herself away from a delightful dream, awakening much too early. But she recalled the patients waiting for her and rose without hesitation. Looking at Marina as she buttoned her coat, she queried, "But when...? How...?"

"After work, return home as usual and explain to your flat mates that you will be spending a few nights with your patient, Niki. Gather some belongings and return here. We will spend some days catechizing you and determining the best course for your well-being, with help from our priest, Fr. Daniil. He is wise and gifted at navigating these troubled waters well, to keep his flock safe. For now, go with the blessing of God, and the prayers of our Xenia. I will tell *Batiushka*+ all." Marina made the sign of the cross upon Lena's head as though she were a child, and embraced and kissed her, gently pushing her out the door.

◆|✷|✷|✷|◆

Walking to the bus stop, Yelena was carried by a powerful sense of joy and elation, such that she had never felt in her life before. It superseded even the delight of falling in love with Sasha. Colors seemed more vivid, sounds more sweet, and each face she saw seemed infinitely dear. *They are all created by Him; they all bear His image, every one*, she thought to herself, awestruck. She breathed the pure air in deeply, casting her eyes upward to the fluttering leaves and prayed silently: *Dearest God of all, thank you for reaching me. I cannot imagine how I could have strayed so far from you, how I could have forgotten. But thank you for believing in me. And Blessed Xenia, your prayers, I know, helped to bring me back. Thank you, thank you!*

Thoughts tumbled through Yelena's mind on the bus ride, each competing for her attention. It was as if her mind could not catch up with what her heart already knew. *Where*

+ Formal title for a priest; i.e. "Father."

was Sasha? Would he come back now? Were any of her colleagues at the hospital Christian? What could she say if asked about religious belief? How would things change at work? What if Ivan and Tanya found out?

Yelena sighed and closed her eyes. She slipped into a state of half-wakefulness and faces swam before her eyes: Sasha's look of endearment that she knew so well and longed for now, Niki's hopeful smile, Mama's eyes full of devotion in the candlelight, Vanya's drunken leer, Marina's keen appraisal, her colleague's cold calculation before a diagnosis, those clear green eyes piercing to her very soul from a disheveled beggar.... Yelena's eyes burst open as the bus lurched to a stop. Why did she remember that beggar now? Perhaps because she understood more clearly what he had seen, or rather, had failed to see in her, that day.

She disembarked and followed the crowd up wide concrete steps into the hospital. Perfunctorily turning to the staircase, she pushed open the heavy door and let it fall back into place with a gentle swoosh. It was her habit to avoid the elevator, even though she worked on the 6th floor. As always, the staircase chamber echoed resonantly. Instead of the usual clipping of heels and thunks of doors, Yelena heard a conversation taking place.

"...but honestly, what would you have me do? She's under my supervision, yes, but I can't be responsible for foolish things she does on her own time," a frustrated senior doctor complained.

"Karl, you know it's not that simple. At this point, this is a very serious accusation. If she's a believer, it must be dealt with, nipped in the bud. If she doesn't heed your warning, I'd extricate myself if I were you – fail to renew her placement contract on some technicality if you don't want to put her forth to the authorities. It could come back to haunt you, you know. Don't just pretend it's not there."

Yelena stopped in her tracks, stunned. She knew who

was speaking. Karl Dolinsky, a pediatrician renowned for his work with genetic disorders, had been one of a team evaluating her projects and exams before her medical certification. And the second doctor, an obstetrician, was someone she knew in passing.

"What's the worst they could do, really? I'm two years from retirement," Karl reasoned.

"Didn't you hear what happened to Antipoff last month?"

"What? the surgeon with that crazy Christian wife of his? Wasn't her father a priest or something? What does it matter? He's always been a good communist. Never heard a superstitious word from him."

"Yes, but after years of warning, they finally officially charged him – and he's completely lost his pension package, and virtually all his savings in fines. Plus, he was terminated eight months early."

"What?!" Karl exclaimed incredulously. "But how is that possible?! What could he have possibly done to merit such a severe ruling?"

"The state considers it a fair alternative to imprisonment in their old age. She's been openly taking their grandchildren to church for years, and..."

"That may be stupid, but it's hardly against the law!" interrupted Karl.

"It most certainly is! You haven't been keeping up with the news, eh? Kruschev's ban on taking children to Protestant churches was recently extended three months ago to Orthodox churches as well. If they're over 4 years old, it's now officially a crime. And as you know, there are plenty of prying eyes and tattling tongues to implicate the rebels. I'm sure there are thousands of unhappy *babushkas* all over the country right now," the obstetrician chuckled.

"What a stupid law – we are Russian, for Christ's sake, and if anything let the old folks go to their graves with their crumbling Orthodoxy. Who cares? The young ones aren't idiot enough to follow suit, especially with the solid education they're now getting from the youngest age. But Antipoff – how can that be? He's faithfully served for decades, and it was his wife's doing, not his! I just can't believe it! What a waste."

"Yeah, 'collusion' and 'abetting' and the like. As I said, Karl, you'd better talk to your underling. She's playing with fire, and for what, a fantasy? It will not only curtail her own career, but it may affect yours as well, even at this late stage. The government is cracking down again, and you don't want to be anywhere near that terrible frenzy of suspicion," he replied, opening the door to their destination. "You remember what it's like."

Both men sighed heavily, recalling earlier years of harsh religious persecution and how it tore apart the fabric of neighborhoods and families. The recent reprieve after World War II, in which much greater religious freedom was allowed, was apparently ending.

"Well, I suppose you're right," Karl conceded. "Although it's hard to see the individual lives ruined, in the bigger picture Mother Russia has got to shake off this cancerous love affair with delusion. And sometimes the incisive surgery, though deep, is better than surface treatments that don't get the job done. Antipoff should have put an end to his wife's ridiculousness years ago, though. Can you imagine having to live the rest of your life off charity..." The voices trailed off and Yelena heard the soft thud of the door closing.

Sinking to the stair below her, she sat with her head in her hands, realizing that this could be a future conversation about her. *What am I doing? Am I crazy?* Doubt plagued her, and the situation seemed impossible, untenable. Tears of frustration began to spring up as Yelena struggled to gain her composure. She was already terribly late. How could she possibly pretend that nothing had happened in front of all her colleagues, and go about her day seeming to be as one with them, after all she had realized. It felt like she would be living a lie.

If God is all they say He is, why does He allow such a situation as this? Why does he allow His faithful people to be persecuted unfairly? And how can any of them – Marina, Sasha, Xenia, God – how can they expect me to figure this out all by myself? It isn't fair, and I don't want it!

Hot tears continued to flow as the strong emotions of the last week – anxiety, frustration, relief, bewilderment, joy, hope – all collided within her. Yelena felt lonely at the bottom of it all. She resented Sasha's leaving her here alone to figure it all out. For a few moments, she cried like a little girl in the stairwell, giving vent to her childish emotions.

After a brief moment, she stopped, considered, and took another step forward into herself. *"Jesus, Son of God, if my life is to be given over to You, then let it begin now, and with my whole heart. O Heavenly King, the Comforter, the Spirit of Truth,..."* she silently prayed, amazed at how easily the words of a childhood prayer returned to her. *"...Who art everywhere present and fillest all things,... fill me now. Fill me with your own wisdom. I don't know what to do. I don't know how to do this. If it is what You're asking of me, then You must do it for me. I give You my job, my education, my love for Sasha, everything I have. It is Yours to do with as You will. Enlighten my heart and mind. Come, Lord Jesus, be with me; Holy Mother of God, guide me in all my thoughts and actions, through the prayers of Blessed Xenia and all the saints. Amen."*

Yelena sighed, peace rising within her. She stood and straightened her skirt, drying her eyes and smoothing her hair. The day passed as it always did. No one remarked upon the subtle changes in Yelena: to everyone else, it was just a normal day.

CHAPTER XIV

St. Petersburg, 1761

Xenia had continued to come and go from the house unannounced for some time. Apart from the strange outburst prophesying the advent of Paraskeva's new son, Xenia was more often unobtrusive and quiet; sometimes the only sign she had been in the house was a menial task completed which Paraskeva had left undone. Paraskeva didn't know where she went, where she slept if she was out at night, nor what she ate, since she seldom had any food, even though Paraskeva offered her nourishment every chance she got, often saving the tastiest morsels for her friend, to no avail. The soldier's uniform stood at attention in the drawing room, pressed and starched, ever since she had asked for it. It almost felt as if Andre were present with them again every time she passed the open door. Paraskeva had heard and understood her friend's request to be left to her devotions, and therefore she asked no questions and did her best to preserve Xenia's newfound inner life undisturbed.

After a time, Xenia finally sat down with Paraskeva for a cup of hot tea and she began to share with her oldest and dearest friend what she had seen, what she had experienced, and what she had encountered during her eight long years of exile. There was an eloquence and decisiveness in her tone that Paraskeva noticed, as if Xenia had meticulously recorded and contemplated all that she said, as if it had all sunk into her very bones.

After a long conversation, Xenia suddenly got up from the chair she was sitting in, and without explanation she slowly, methodically, began donning Andrei's regimental uniform, piece by piece. First, she put on the underwear and the striking red hose, then the finely-tailored linen overshirt and pantaloons which had fit Andrei perfectly, but looked like an oversized sack on Xenia's slight frame. Finally, she put on the felt shoes, several sizes too big for her feet, and the elegant, skirted green coat with its bright red cuffs and shining copper buttons. She stood ensconced in the entire uniform that her beloved Andrei had loved so much while he was alive, looking like a comical caricature, or a child playing at dress-up. Her face, however, bore an expression of sobriety that bespoke anything but a joke.

Paraskeva stared at her friend while she did this, utterly perplexed. Despite herself, she even entertained a passing concern about the mental state of her dear Xenia: was she quite well?

"I can't understand, my dearest, why you are putting on your beloved Andrei's clothes," she said, with a sincere show of concern. Glancing at the pile of discarded gray, threadbare wraps heaped on the floor, she continued, "If it is because you need new clothes, I still have the clothing you left in the armoire upstairs."

"No; do not trouble yourself. My dear sister and friend of my heart," Xenia answered, looking at her intently with a level eye, "the reason I am wearing my dear Andrei's clothes, is because from this day forward, you must accept that I have ceased to be Xenia!"

After her strange and unusual response, Paraskeva noticed a change flicker across Xenia's countenance. Whereas during the ceremony of dressing, there had been firm resolution, now there was a faint glow upon her face, and a softening of the features that seemed to be not of this world.

Xenia continued with a deliberate and authoritative tone, "From now on, I must be known as Andrei Theodorovich Petrov! I will not answer to any other name."

"But why?" asked Paraskeva, unable to suppress the obvious question, both confused and concerned at Xenia's disturbing proclamation.

"Because I must cease to be Xenia Grigorievna – that is how it must be; it is my path. God, in His mercy, is allowing any humiliations I will suffer by wearing this uniform to be Andrei's humiliations, borne through me. When Andrei died, his earthly experiences in this world ceased, so there was no way he could do anything more for the benefit of his eternal condition. Andrei might no longer be in this world, but I am, and therefore I must substitute myself for him. It will be as if he still exists in this world, for *he* will be suffering the humiliations that I encounter. My sacrifices from here on in will be for his spiritual benefit, and in God's perfect wisdom, also for my own."

As Xenia was explaining this, the earnest and peaceful expression on her face and her unhesitating will to do such a thing overwhelmed Paraskeva, for it reflected sheer purity and the great expansiveness of Xenia's love. This love that emanated from Xenia was not only for her late husband Andrei, but also for her friend Paraskeva, and for all of humanity. It was shining from her face; it was palpable. It was a love that transcended this world, and it was formed out of a heart wounded by pain. Not only did Xenia feel the pain of losing her beloved spouse, but she also felt the more profound pain of anxiety over the dreadful eternal state her husband was in, due to his untimely death and the profligate life he led prior to it.

Throughout her long exile Xenia concerned herself only with Andrei and the agony he was in, the memory of his early pleas for help resounding in her ears. She contemplated on it day and night as she walked from place to place. "How can our Lord redeem someone, unless they themselves are willing to accept the need for that redemption?" Xenia would think sorrowfully, as her tears flowed for her poor late husband.

Xenia's long personal journey was not only one of private prayer, but also one in which she sought spiritual counsel from monastic wisdom. On this journey, she was enlightened about the sin of Andrei's pride and that it had to be diminished somehow.

"Without repentance at the time of death, a soul can only exist in a darkened state, separated from the love of God, an unfortunate and depressing state: 'hell,' with all its dreadful connotations. Without a chance for repentance, how can a person find his way back to our Lord's love?" Xenia wondered, shuddering at the thought. Xenia's earthly love for Andrei had now deepened into a spiritual love with her fervent prayers: a much purer, much dearer love. She reflected that she would do whatever earthly thing it might take in order to redeem him.

The thought of dressing as Andrei, taking on his persona, was not born out of impulse, but was an illumination that dawned upon her over time. During Xenia's extraordinary spiritual education among the holy elders and eldresses in the many corners of Russia she visited, she had learned about the struggle towards salvation, and little by little, she was prepared by them to take the great leap forward in this struggle that was before her now. She had learned about Orthodoxy's "holy fools" – saints throughout centuries and locales who had put on, as it were, the garb of foolishness in order to attain humility. They had appeared strange to those around them by living in trees, caves or on pillars, ceasing to speak or speaking incessantly in riddles, living destitute and homeless by choice, refusing to eat but only a few items, or eating meat flagrantly during the holy periods of abstinence. These stories had planted a seed, which God nurtured in her.

It was with this revealed knowledge that she bravely and assuredly put on all the brilliant attire of her husband's proud regiment, so that she could diminish his pride with her selfless action. And in so doing, Xenia knew that she would further her own soul's preparation for the Heavenly Kingdom.

◆I✳I✳I✳I◆

Looking quite foolish in a man's military uniform a few sizes too large for her, Xenia took leave of Paraskeva Antonova's home. She closed the door firmly on that past life of waste that she and Andrei had lived together there. Despite the goodness and love of their marriage, and the sweet memories she still had, Xenia knew without a doubt that the purer love she had attained for him over these years of grief and struggle, which he undoubtedly could now appreciate, was worlds better than what they had started with. She closed that door and ventured into the new world which she was to inhabit for the next thirty-seven years. It would be a world of complete servitude and penance in the *Petersburgskaya Storona*, which was perpetually plagued with hunger, floods and disease.

CHAPTER XV

Leningrad, 1963

That evening Yelena returned to Marina's very late, after having phoned about a difficult patient she needed to spend time with. When she arrived, Marina already had the candles lit and began her prayers as soon as Yelena was beside her. Being mentored in the faith by someone as steady and solid as Marina was incredibly comforting. It was the surety and strong hope of Orthodoxy that calmed and grounded her flailing mind, trained as it was to trust empirical evidence above all else.

After falling into bed next to Marina, exhausted, Yelena recalled the events of the day and the difficult moments in the stairwell. Again, she thought of Sasha. But now, with her heart softened by prayer, instead of anger and resentment, she only felt deep sadness.

"Marishka," she said softly in the dark, "why did Sasha leave me? Why didn't he tell me about it?" A tear slid silently down her cheek.

"My dove, he was afraid; and he sacrificed his own desires for love. Do you understand? He loved you so dearly, yet at the same time he knew that the temporal is as nothing, compared to the eternal. He chose to give you the gift of your own free will." Again, Lena marveled at the deep philosophy of her peasant bedfellow.

Marina continued, "Sasha was afraid to tell you – afraid to lose you, or to hurt you. He did not know how you would react. He also didn't want to burden you with sensitive information, or put you in a position of being pressed to make a choice on his behalf. For him, the rekindling of faith happened rather quickly, as it has for you. It was only a few times of seeing him hiding in the shadows of our little prayer services at Blessed Xenia's grave before he approached us and asked to be received."

"I see. It makes some sense to me, and I hadn't considered what difficult choices it put before him," she responded. "But I am still amazed at how I could not have known all this was going on within him."

"Well, remember you had not seen one another for nearly a month before he made himself known to us. He was beside himself with worry about it for several days," said Marina. "But finally by asking me to reach out to you and considering *Batiushka's* counsel, he saw his way clear. Things fell into place quickly then, by the prayers of Blessed Xenia."

"He asked you to contact me?" Yelena asked.

"Why yes, didn't I mention it before? When I spoke of Niki's young compassionate doctor, he knew at once that it was you. He asked me to request a meeting so that we could meet one another and to provide you with an avenue towards Saint Xenia, if you would take it. And certainly his prayers have also guided you these last weeks."

"Certainly so," replied Yelena. "But what of *Batiushka's* counsel to him?"

"He encouraged Sasha to give you some time and space for your own spiritual journey. Fr. Daniil dissuaded him from going to you before he left, causing a commotion in your life and offering untimely explanations that would only come as a shock to you. This way, you have had time for reflection and questions, and have found your own authentic way back to God, which was Sasha's dearest hope for you."

"But why did he leave, and where did he go?" asked Yelena.

"Sasha, as you know, was close to his cadre of artisans and sculptors here in the workshop. With their constant dialogues on philosophy, beauty, and the like, it would be impossible for him to hide his faith from them. Rather than being denounced and losing his craft, as his brother in Christ has, (Stephan, the street-sweeper who gave you his letter) we thought it better for him to seek a commission in a new locale, where he could begin again as an unknown, and keep his own counsel more closely. He is in the town of Pushkin, just 24 km south of here."

Yelena absorbed all this information as her mind drifted toward sleep. It put her heart at ease to know the ways in which Sasha had continued to love and care for her, even through this painful separation that had taken time for her to understand. *Loving Lord, again I bow to Your holy will. If it is possible, let Sasha and I be together again. But I pray for Your will in our lives more than my own.*

◆❘✳❘✳❘✳❘◆

Yelena pushed herself up the stairs to her flat after another busy day at the hospital. After a full week at Marina's she felt reluctance at arriving back here, even though it was her own home. Ivan and Tanya had been so grateful for a few days to themselves that they didn't even wonder about her departure. But here she was, back again, to prevent any suspicions from cropping up. She heard loud banging and scraping as she approached the door, and opened it with her key cautiously.

"Lena! Here you are!" boomed Ivan. "Tanya! She's home, darling."

Tanya came through the bedroom door with a pile of neatly folded blankets balanced on her pregnant belly, smiling widely. "What do you think, Lena? Our new flat is ready before we even knew it! So you'd better call your sweet Sasha and have him over pronto – the place is yours alone tomorrow night! We're leaving in the morning. Oh, you can stay another night with your patient's grandmother, can't you?"

Yelena suddenly realized that the entire apartment was in shambles, with boxes and bags everywhere. There was no place for her to sleep. She joined Ivan and Tanya in a celebratory toast and reminisced for an hour about their time together. She felt relief at closing the door upon that apartment, and upon that chapter of her life. *Thank you, Blessed Xenia,* she whispered. *You take care of everything.*

As she descended the stairs with a few belongings, Yelena fingered the black woolen prayer rope in her pocket that Marina had given her. She touched the knots one by one, saying, *Lord Jesus Christ, Son of God, have mercy on me.* Reaching the phone downstairs, she dialed.

"I'm coming home again tonight," she said.

"Perfect," replied Marina. "God changed your plans, eh? Well, no wonder. He's got a surprise here for you when you arrive."

◆│✳│✳│✳│◆

Yelena jumped off the final step of the bus with extra sprightliness. She was only slightly ashamed that at her age she still loved surprises so much. Her first thought was that perhaps at long last Sasha had come to see her. By now she surely would know about the unfolding events in her life. Yet she knew a visit was unlikely. He had begun work on an important commission with a strict deadline, and she knew he would be hard at work for some time to complete it.

As she tripped up the now-familiar staircase to Niki and Marina's door, she could hear voices and laughter emanating from above. This was unusual; Marina often entertained friends during the day, but evenings they had always been alone.

She knocked on the door and Niki opened it with excitement, jumping into her arms. He was no longer bed-ridden and had been roaming about the flat for days with increasing strength. "*Batiushka* is here! And Daddy!" he yelled, releasing her as quickly as he had embraced her and pulling her into the room.

Yelena saw two men rising to greet her. The younger, around her own age, with an infectious grin and unruly crop of yellow hair, was a cross of features she already recognized. He had Marina's almond eyes and Niki's wiry build and heart-shaped facial structure. They all three shared the same nose and the same quick, active response to the world around them.

Grasping her forearm, he said warmly, "Yelena. I am so pleased to meet you at last. I am Dimitri, Niki's father. May I present our dear *Batiushka*, Daniil." He guided her toward the other man in the room, whom Yelena had only yet glanced at. She noticed his simple black cassock and wooden cross, focusing on his right hand which was stretched out to bless her.

With heart pattering for fear of doing it wrong, Yelena recalled Marina's coaching. She bowed her head, cupping her hands together and waiting for the priest to rest his hand within them. It all felt very natural to her until the very last moment. After his soft words of blessing, and the gentle pressure of his hand upon her head, she kissed his worn fingers and looked up into the startling green eyes that had haunted her memories and dreams. Here before her in the garb of his true calling was the prophetic beggar who had pierced her heart weeks ago.

Yelena gasped in surprise. "You!" she sputtered awkwardly. "You – you're the one who saw me on the bus!"

"Yes, dear one, I saw you. And I see you now," he replied simply.

◆⌗✳⌗✳⌗◆

It took Yelena some time to regain her composure. Of all the strange happenings and surprising turns, this was the most bewildering to her. It provoked two opposing responses simultaneously. First, it stripped her completely bare of any sense of control or perception. She had been a student of science, trained to observe the unusual. Yet this beggar-priest had completely escaped her recognition, as if she truly had no skill whatsoever. She felt as if she were nothing. Secondly, with this second look into his eyes, she felt a greater warmth and recognition than she had ever felt with any person in her life. She knew instantaneously what it was that she had been unable to comprehend earlier – love. What she had mistakenly interpreted as a judgment of her weaknesses before, she now understood was just love. But what a love it was! Such as she had never known before, at once both intimately personal, transcendent and eternal.

They spent long hours together in that little home, well into the morning. It was overflowing with joy, with the reunion of lost family members and the delight of togetherness in Christ. Niki fell asleep before long in the arms of his father as they stood at prayer – the Akathist to Saint Xenia, in thanksgiving for her faithfulness to them. Dimitri continued to hold his son close through the hours of intense conversation, in which the mysteries of faith were unfolded to Yelena, received deeply into her being.

They discussed her situation and how best to approach these changes. It was decided that she should continue her formative work at the hospital, keeping her devotions hidden from all but the few believers they knew of who worked there: another female doctor and a handful of nurses and aides. Being in an environment that was largely academic and cerebral had its blessings. Discussions of moral, spiritual, and even psychological issues were not commonplace and attracted no attention if one chose to step away from them. Yelena was not particularly close to anyone beyond professional respect, and her new faith would not be easily detectable by anyone.

A secret baptism would be arranged for her after another week or two of tutelage under Marina. Having been whisked into a world of liturgics and interior prayer, of ecclesiastical history, lives of the saints and hierarchical etiquette, Yelena felt she had learned a tremendous amount in a short time. Indeed, she had. But she was amazed to hear *Batiushka* and Marina discuss the topics she had not yet been educated about: hymnography and feast days, iconography and architecture, fasting and acts of mercy. Fr. Daniil explained that these were the "trappings" or "traditions" of Orthodox Christianity, the human experience of it.

"But you, my dear child, will also enter into the essence of our faith, the Presence of our Lord Himself, and His illumination through the lives of those who love Him – both those who have gone before, like our Blessed Xenia, and those of us who struggle here now, the community of believers, imperfect though we be. And this all starts here," he said, touching his breast, "in the *nous*[+], or the heart, if you will. It starts with your own relationship with Him and your life of prayer with Him. I can see for myself that you have already begun."

[+] A Greek word denoting the highest spiritual faculty, denoting rationality, intelligence and conscience; usually imperfectly translated as "heart" in English.

◆❚✳❚✳❚✳❚◆

The conversation finally came near to the end. Although it was the wee hours of the night, all were still infused with spiritual energy and fully engaged with the miracle they all felt was occurring among them. They ended with a final prayer together and a whispered hymn before the icons, which Marina had taken out from their hiding place. As he rose from his knees to depart, and before Yelena had a chance to ask the final question of her heart, Fr. Daniil said, "And now, my dear one, the final thing to discuss, in its proper place, is the question of your beloved. Do you still wish to marry Sasha, after all that has occurred, or do you need more time to consider this question?" He looked at her searchingly.

Yelena needed no time to consider. "*Batiushka*, it is the dearest wish of my heart, apart from pleasing my Lord throughout the rest of my life."

"Amen," he replied. "Then so be it. Sasha has said the same. We will arrange for the wedding to take place immediately after your baptism. You understand, it cannot be a grand affair, and you will have to go through the motions of a secular union soon after to keep up appearances. But we will serve the sacraments together quietly in a forgotten church I have in mind during the night. Afterwards, you will be able to return together to your flat, which I understand is now ready for your life together. I'm afraid Sasha will be coming and going for some time, until he can re-establish himself on better footing here in Saint Petersburg, but I imagine you will hardly mind a little inconvenience, with the richness of blessings God has bestowed upon you."

CHAPTER XVI

Saint Petersburg, 1761 - 1798

Having fully assumed her new identity as Andrei, Xenia began roaming the shabby streets of Saint Matthew's Parish of the *Peterburgskaya Storona*. She was firmly determined to help the poor in whichever way she could, and to make sure that every blessing received through her charity and deeds would not be given to her, but rather to Andrei. All would soon learn that Xenia would only answer to her dead husband's name.

"Look at that crazy woman," the street urchins would cry, as she walked along the streets.

"Ha! Look at how silly she is. She is wearing a man's uniform!"

"Hey, don't you know?" shouted one sarcastically. "That is Colonel Andrei Theodorovich Petrov! Hahaha!"

"Hey, Andrei, Andrei! Why don't you sing for us," another urchin cried to her tauntingly. And with that, they all began to chant in a ridiculous, exaggerated fashion, mimicking the music and sounds of the esteemed Imperial Choristers.

"How handsome you look in your fancy uniform! Isn't that the uniform of the *Preobrazhensky Regiment*?" they jeered, strutting stiffly, pretending to be royal guards.

"It fits you so nicely Andrei, but I didn't know that you were a woman," another called out in derision. They all burst into raucous laughter.

"Yeah, yeah, and look how nice and clean it is – but we will change that," they yelled, picking up fistfuls of mud from the street and throwing it at her.

Xenia ignored the taunting, and prayed for Andrei, and for the children who jeered, but nevertheless, a tear rolled down her cheek silently.

The young ruffians, in their thoughtlessness, were trying to humiliate the nobility and grandeur that was so far from their reach. They never thought to themselves that there was a human being created in the image of God beneath the uniform they were assaulting.

After having finished with their sarcastic insults and malicious harassments, the scalliwags, who were thoroughly enjoying themselves, trailed away with casual laughter to find other sport, having failed to provoke a response. They knew that they could do and say whatever they wanted without any impediment, and that even the Royal Guards themselves would not stop them – they were never seen in this neighborhood. But for her part, Xenia determined that for their next meeting, she would have some bread tucked away to give them. The bare feet, thin frames and protruding cheek bones did not escape her notice.

◆❘✳❘✳❘✳❘◆

Relentless harassment on the streets towards Xenia and her husband's prestigious uniform went on for months, not only from children, but from grown men and women as well. The *Preobrazhensky Regiment* was reserved for nobility only. Class structure was very pronounced in this world. Such a uniform proclaimed to all not only prestige, respect and honor, (being the most honored of all the guards), but free access to all the royal palaces and deferential treatment from the top echelons of society. Xenia's humiliating choice to roam the poorest streets as a "fool for Christ" dressed in this manner was breaking all the socially-accepted rules and norms of class behavior. It scandalized many. And it cast a spiritually penetrating light on the wide gulf between the "haves" and the "have-nots."

Nevertheless, Saint Xenia continued to walk about and silently pray in the streets of the *Petersburgskaya Storona*. Never forgetting that the reviling degradation she was suffering was, in reality, to Andrei's spiritual benefit, Xenia often stopped to openly bless those who were humiliating her in her husband's name. Only a few responded with a softening of heart, initially; most were perplexed by her odd behavior and it even increased their fervor in taunting her.

Since they failed to get the response from Xenia that they were expecting, and being overtaken by their sinful and hateful passions, a few began to act out even more aggressively. Xenia, as usual, tried to ignore them as best she could outwardly, while inwardly she blessed them and prayed for their souls and well-being in the name of the servant of God, Andrei Theodorovich Petrov.

The intractable behavior eventually turned malicious and even escalated one day to a group of young hooligans throwing stones at poor Xenia. *Whack!* the heavy stone resounded, as its rough edges grazed Xenia painfully across the hand, tearing off some skin. *Thunk!* resounded another smaller one as it hit her cheek, narrowly missing her eye. Mud and dirt was one thing; this was quite another. Xenia knew that if she were hurt physically, she would not be able to continue all the works of charity that she intended to carry out. So, in this particular instance, she had the incentive, as well as the fortitude of will and God's blessing, to defend herself.

Rather than look aside in meekness, this time the "fool for Christ" took the taunting gang by surprise, and with a resolve they had not seen before, she turned and ran after them, shaking her old but sturdy cane in the air! Intended to warn them off rather than truly harm them, the surprising effort made her point nonetheless.

Xenia's unexpected response was a blessing in disguise, since it finally aroused the dormant sympathy of her good neighbors. A group of women watching from the storefront nearby and a few men smoking pipes at a table across the way observed the incident. The men burst into laughter while the women cheered her on. They had all had been the target of the unruly gang's recreations on a lonely street at night. It brought Xenia's many sufferings, which they had largely ignored, to their attention. They began to see Xenia in a different light, and little by little, most of them began to consider her one of their own, different though she might be.

The devout inhabitants of Saint Petersburg, and more especially the poor of Saint Matthias' parish, at length began to realize the extent of Xenia's holiness. They came to understand, through her enduring acts of mercy, that she was not insane, but that she was well within the fullness of God's grace. She was not only willing to suffer for her deceased husband's soul, but she also wanted to help all she encountered in any way she could. One by one, the grateful residents began to invite Blessed Xenia into their homes.

It did not take long, in fact, for her neighbors to notice that whenever they asked blessed Xenia to visit them, this kindness would be repaid back a thousand-fold. Blessings upon them would abound: a business owner would see his sales boom, a mother with a sick child blessed by the old woman would see him get well immediately, an inconsolable baby would calm down and remain at peace throughout the day, and a man drowning in debt would receive unexpected funds.

In time, and as a result of these miracles becoming known throughout the area, everyone began competing for Xenia's visits. This would become especially true of the cab drivers in the city. Not only would they refuse to accept money from her, but they would stop their cabs, begging her to come and ride with them! Even if Xenia rode in a cab for only a few feet, that particular cab driver's fares would skyrocket for the rest of that day!

Later in her life, a decision was made to construct a beautiful church on the grounds of the *Smolensky Cemetery*. In those days labor was mostly manual and exhaustive. Imagine the relief and delight the day's bricklayers must have felt when they arrived at the jobsite at sunrise one morning to find hundreds of bricks all neatly stacked high atop the scaffolding, ready for laying. "This is fantastic! What a blessing someone has given us!" a young man said to his older colleague.

"What?!" he replied. "Then it wasn't you who carried all these bricks up here? Who did, then?"

The mystery deepened as, day after day, the bricks would be found assembled and waiting. No matter how early they came, they could not catch the benevolent helpers. The laborers' increasing bewilderment eventually piqued the interest of the supervisors, who took it upon themselves to discover who was aiding this work so impressively without regard for pay.

Unable to discover anything by their interviews of workers and neighboring folk alike, they finally posted secret guards at night. Lo and behold, it was the Blessed Xenia! No one could have guessed that an aged woman was responsible for such an impressive amount of work alone in the dead of night. She showed a physical strength and fortitude far beyond what anyone could imagine her possessing; indeed it was only by the grace of God and her own sheer joy at helping to build the holy place that Xenia continued to labor nightly during the construction, hauling hundreds and thousands of bricks up steps and ladders to lay them where they were needed.

◆|✳|✳|✳|◆

Xenia had attained spiritual heights that could no longer be hidden; her humility, her sacrifice, her disassociation with worldly cares and mortal pride, and her unceasing prayer helped her to reach a state of release from the limitations of this world, and thus, she was gifted by God with many spiritual *charismata*.⁺ Through the purity of her heart, Saint Xenia was graced with the ability to read the souls of others, as well as the power to heal the sick and to tell of future events. Xenia's charismatic graces were soon to become known far and wide among the inhabitants of Saint Petersburg and beyond.

⁺ Spiritual gifts which often supersede expected perceptions or skills, such as foreknowledge of events, or the ability to understand a language one does not know.

CHAPTER XVII

EPILOGUE

St. Petersburg, 2002

The crowd around the chapel had abated, leaving just a few straggling pilgrims and one or two young couples searching for secluded spots in which to be alone. Yelena wandered into the cemetery, and found a bench near the walkway shaded by a thick stand of trees. The stone bench was cool. It was August, warm and humid. Many of the visitors she had seen walking about were wearing short sleeves and sandals, but Yelena was feeling her age. She was often cold now. Slipping into the hooded raincoat she had brought against the very likely chance of rain, she waited.

Smolensky Cemetery had been getting some much-needed attention in recent years. The Cathedral of the Smolensk Mother of God, whose feast day was the reason for the crowds, wore a fresh coat of azure blue paint. Acres of the lush, verdant plant life that had once grown so wild and carefree had been somewhat tamed by skilled groundskeepers. Timber-edged paths meandered alongside well-tended graves adorned by masses of petunias, geraniums, and live-forever. Most of the grave-crosses, once forlornly crumbled and broken, were now repaired, fittingly adorning the gravestones as beacons of hope. Amidst the surrounding foliage, the green stone chapel that had served as Sasha's workshop was nestled like a fern.

"Lena?"

Yelena whirled around, startled out of her reverie. The tall blond man who had called her name held out his hand to help her to her feet. Then he kissed her on both cheeks.

"Niki!" She held him by the arms, looking into his hazel eyes. "My goodness, are you still growing?"

"I don't think so, unless you mean here," Nikolai laughed, patting his stomach. "I'm pretty sure most men are finished growing by the time they're my age. You're the pediatrician, what do you think?"

"I didn't remember you being so tall. You seem to have grown six inches since I was here a year ago. I must be shrinking in my old age."

"Has it really been a year since you've been to St. Petersburg?"

"I like hearing Leningrad called by that name, but it's hard for me to get used to," Yelena said. "It was when your grandmother died. That was the last time I was here. A year ago this month, wasn't it?"

"Yes, it was," Nikolai said, crossing himself. But, you've seen me since then. We came to Troitska in May, for the feast day of St. Helen, remember? We saw the icon of her that Papa had just finished."

"Of course. And how are my grandchildren? Behaving themselves, I hope."

"You'll see for yourself; Grusha and Katya were 'helping' your daughter prepare the food when I left. Consequently, dinner may not be up to Marina's usual standards." They laughed together, remembering the lovingly-prepared and delicious dishes with which dear Marina had nourished them all, even upon her scant budget. "My car is parked across from the cathedral, where is...?"

"Out there somewhere," Yelena said, waving her hand in the general direction her husband had gone. She took Nikolai's arm and they walked out into one of the older sections that had yet to be conquered by the cemetery's gardeners. It was a dark, secluded area where the dense forest crown was nearly closed against the light and many of the monuments had acquired a *verdigris* patina.[+]

After a few minutes of wandering around the graves, Yelena spotted her husband standing near an ancient vault headed by a towering stone cross. Sasha's hair was still dark at seventy-five but threaded with silver, and he was dressed in his priest's cassock. Grouped around him were eight or ten darkly-clad young people in their late teens and early twenties, curiously attentive to him. Their appearance, although becoming more commonplace in the larger cities, still startled Yelena: silver piercings in places they seemed least likely to belong, studded buckles and ostentatious metallic jewelry, dressed all in black, often with fringe, leather or chains. Both boys and girls wore garish, dramatic makeup: pasty faces accented by black-rimmed eyes and blood-red lips, framed by long, bleached-white or raven-black hair. Popularly referred to as Goths, they belonged to the Neo-Pagan subculture spreading throughout St. Petersburg in recent years. These young people probably found the *Smolensky Cemetery's* dappled gloom a proper mood-setter for their strange attraction to death and darkness.

"Look there, Niki," Yelena said, with unabashed admiration for her charismatic and open-hearted husband, "*Batiushka* has found someone to talk with about our beloved Saint Xenia."

[+] A "true green coating," covered in a light moss or lichen.

CHAPTER XVI

EPILOGUE

The Miracles and Charismata of Saint Xenia

Xenia was a light in the darkened streets and palace hallways of Imperial Russia. Like the great saints of old, Xenia had a *podvig*⁺, given by God, which she chose to embrace. For others it was martyrdom, loss, persecution, or monasticism. For Xenia, it was to be a fool in the eyes of the world, a fool for Christ's sake. After years of lonely labors, this penetrating act of faith on her part, combined with God's grace, gifted her with spiritual adornments which could not be hidden. People in her lifetime sought her out for help and guidance. And after her death, her fame spread throughout the entire world, continuing to this day.

◆❘✴❘✴❘✴❘◆

⁺ An arduous task or labor which results in spiritual gain.

During her lifetime, frequent miracles occurred through Xenia. In the year 1761 Blessed Xenia returned to Saint Petersburg after living as an ascetic[+] and wandering as a pilgrim for eight years. Two days before Christmas, Xenia ran through the streets crying anxiously and excitedly: "Bake, *bliny*,[‸] bake *bliny*, for soon all of Russia will be baking *bliny!*"

Since the small pancakes were only baked when someone died, the residents of the *Petersburgskaya Storona* were confused by Xenia's outbursts. Not fully understanding her spiritual *charism* and her gift of clairvoyance,[*] some became frightened, fearing that someone they knew had died or would die. Naturally, there were others that interpreted her ranting as that of a mad woman:

"Surely she must be insane," a few of them would say. "Why is she telling us to bake *bliny*?"

"Look at her," others would cry, shaking their heads in disgust. "She is running around like a crazy woman, wearing a man's uniform, spouting ridiculous orders. What will she come up with next?"

But two days after Xenia's frantic calls for *bliny*, the Empress of all Russia, Elizabeth Petrovna, died. This prophetic cry from the lips of a "fool" was only one occurrence of a gift that was manifested many times by our dear saint. But it was a moment which caught the attention

---

[+] One who denounces pleasures and luxuries to live a life of austerity in pursuit of spiritual gain.

[‸] Small dairy-rich pancakes traditionally made for a funeral and the weekend before Lent begins.

[*] The charism (spiritual gift) of clairvoyance is to perceive facts, events or inner realities not usually observable to others. Sometimes, as in this instance, the gifted person knows of events that will happen in the future.

of many and began to change the people's perception of this "crazy woman" in their midst.

Another occasion of this gift was when she paid her dear friend, Mrs. Golubev, a visit. Saint Xenia was quite fond of the widow's lovely daughter because she had a warm and tender heart. As the girl was helping her mother offer hospitality by pouring a cup of coffee, Saint Xenia said to her excitedly: "My beautiful, beautiful child, here you are making coffee for me when your poor husband is burying his wife in Okhta. Run there quickly!"

The girl was shocked! "My what?" she asked. "I don't have a husband! Burying his wife...? Whatever can you mean?"

"Go!" said Xenia sternly, never being one to accept objections.

The Golubevs had known Saint Xenia for many years, and they knew that she would never say anything foolishly, so they immediately put on their coats and made their way to Okhta. At their arrival, they happened upon a funeral procession and solemnly joined in with the mourners. Inquiring whose funeral this was, they were told that the young wife of a doctor had just died in childbirth. They proceeded with the mourners after the service to the cemetery.

The woman was soon buried and everyone began to leave, full of sorrow. The Golubevs, too, were following the crowd out when they chanced to look back at the husband, who had been given some privacy and last moments with his deceased wife. Strangely enough, they realized that the grieving young widower had actually fainted and was lying unconscious upon the grave. They ran over to him swiftly and nursed him back to consciousness. Comforting him in his sorrow with words of faith in God's eternal mercy and his wife's blessed departure to Paradise, the young woman with kind eyes caught his attention. Over the months to come, he came to realize that God had gifted his poor motherless child with a perfect substitute as surely as He had also given the ideal companion of the young doctor's heart. In due time the young woman became his wife, thus fulfilling Saint Xenia's prophesy.

Other instances of foreknowledge were also recorded amongst the many miracles wrought during Xenia's life. She was heard warning loudly about "blood flowing" three weeks before the assassination of Emperor Ivan VI in 1764, whose unfortunate life was lost in a coup by the Empress Elizabeth.

One night in 1796, Xenia walked again through the streets calling out: "Bake *bliny*! Bake *bliny*! All must bake *bliny*!" She tapped loudly on windowpanes and insistently commanded the attention of onlookers, pronouncing a crucial event. Two days later, the Great Catherine, renowned Empress of all of the Russias, was dead.

This foreknowledge of future events was a *charism* given to Saint Xenia so that her holiness might be revealed. In time, nothing she said was taken lightly by the people who knew her. When God endows these prophetic gifts to extremely pious individuals like Saint Xenia, He is helping our faith by confirming to us that there is indeed a power that extends beyond human understanding. By allowing us to see Saint Xenia's holiness, He is giving us an understanding and knowledge of what we must do in order to attain an eternity within His love and blessing.

◆❘✶❘✶❘✶❘◆

Known by some for these more spectacular miracles even during her lifetime, Xenia was however most revered for her quiet, faithful presence in Saint Petersburg and her constant acts of mercy for the people there. It was very common to glimpse the forlorn figure on her knees in a field just outside the city, where she loved to pray, and to receive her warm, cheering smile or helping hand in times of need. Those who felt her presence amongst their poor neighborhoods – the places so often neglected by the powerful and influential of St. Petersburg – felt as if they had their own royalty, in the garb of a beggar, traversing their byways and caring for them like a loving mother.

She was known to walk the streets in the lonely hours, especially in the *Petersburgskaya Storona*, keeping watch over the poorest of the poor as they slept. "There goes Blessed Xenia," a young mother might say, looking out her frosty window while rocking her troubled child back to sleep. "She belongs to God, not to this world."

She was seen day after day, month after month, year after year, in constant prayer for the inhabitants of the city, wearing tattered cast-offs. When the clothing of her late husband Andrei gave out, Xenia dressed only in worn rags with a dirty headscarf tied over her hair, her shoes usually in great disrepair, worn without stockings even through the frigid Russian winters. Bronze pennies which she collected from those who could spare a few, she distributed among the poor. The only other gift she would accept from the many who tried to help her was a meager bit of food. It is thought that she slept in an open field at night, braving the elements, and spending most of those hours awake at prayer.

Rather than detesting her poverty and lack of comforts, Xenia seemed to delight in the Cross she willingly bore for the sake of her husband's and her own salvation. Upon entering a house or shop, she would often announce delightedly: "Here is all of me!"

◆❘�܃❘✜❘✜❘✜❘◆

Even after her death, Xenia was a sure help to those in

need. People who had loved and revered her in life continued to ask for assistance even after her death, and often received miraculous healings and help. This is the reason her fame has swept across the world and endured for over 200 years.

Saint Xenia died around 1800 at the age of 71. Although no details about her death, including the day and year, have been preserved, we know that she was laid to rest in the *Smolensk Cemetery*, near the blessed church which her hands had helped to erect. For the people who knew and loved her, this was a tragic loss, however they understood that death is not a separation for those who believe. Pilgrimages[+] to her gravesite began almost immediately after her death. And so many began to take a bit of earth from her grave, that it had to be replenished every year. Even when a stone slab was placed, the pious would chip away pieces to take as a blessing so that over time it, too, disappeared.

Blessed Xenia often appeared in a vision to those who called upon her. She would offer help in difficulties and give warnings, especially to those in desperate situations or great suffering. Many people receiving such a blessing would recount it in writing, making known the deeds from beyond the grave that Blessed Xenia had done.

One such instance was recorded about an unfortunate civil servant named Nicholas Selivanivich Golovin, who came to St. Petersburg in 1907 to put his affairs in order. With many difficulties at work and a mother and two sisters depending on him for their livelihood, he had fallen into a deep despair. Everything seemed impossible to him – he felt he had failed and could see no way out of his terrible troubles. Despite being a faithful Christian believer, dark and troubled ideas of ending things once and for all stole

---

[+] A holy journey undertaken in devotion, usually with the destination being a sacred site or structure.

into his mind.

Walking along the Neva River, Nicholas contemplated throwing himself into the icy waters and surrendering his life, which seemed to him so pitiful, so burdensome. But before his thoughts had progressed to action, he looked up to find an woman standing before him whom he had never seen before. She was dressed in simple, peasant clothing and looked like she was perhaps a poor nun.

"Why are you so sad?" she asked with both tenderness and authority. "Go to the *Smolensk Cemetery* and serve a *panikhida*[+] for Xenia. Everything will come around right for you. Remember your faith."

As suddenly as she had appeared, the woman was gone. Golovin indeed fulfilled the commands of his benefactress, who with her perfect timing and words of action was able to save his very life. Indeed, his affairs were settled better than he could have wished for and Nicholas returned home to his family a changed man with renewed faith and better prospects than he could have imagined.

In another instance, as a young man and heir to the throne, the would-be Emperor Alexander III once contracted a serious case of typhus in the late 1800's. The fever continued rising, accompanied by a spreading red rash, terrible joint pain and delirium. Those around him began to fear for his life, as many died from this illness in those days.

Seeing the Emperor's wife, Grand Duchess Maria Feodorovna, leaving the room of her husband in tears, a palace servant approached her, saying, "Forgive my intrusion, Your Grace, but if you would like to know of a way to help your husband, I am at your service."

"Oh please, anything, anything! Please tell me what I can do," the distraught wife replied.

[+] A short Orthodox service of prayer for the deceased.

"Many are helped by the intercessions of the Blessed Xenia. I myself was healed from illness by her prayers and the faithful ministrations of my family, who prayed to her on my behalf. I have here a small bit of sacred earth from her grave if you wish to use it..."

Thanking the man for his help, the Grand Duchess placed the blessed soil beneath her husband's pillow immediately, beseeching that Xenia would hear and answer her fervent prayers. That very night, keeping watch at the head of her husband's bed, and continuing to call out in grief and anxiety to the Blessed One, Grand Duchess Maria received a vision of Saint Xenia, who told her that not only would her husband recover, but that a daughter would be born to them before long. The saint furthermore instructed that this child should be named Xenia. Within a short time, all that she predicted became true, and the couple with gladness fulfilled her request, bestowing upon their beloved daughter the name that filled all with hope and gratitude.

◆▮✳▮✳▮✳▮◆

Countless instances like these continue to be manifest in the lives of those who call on Saint Xenia in faith, even in our own day. Many have been healed by her intercessions; many have had their overwhelming problems and dangers resolved by her prayers.

Blessed Xenia was first canonized as a saint officially in the Orthodox Church in 1978.[+] In 1902 a chapel was built over her grave in the *Smolensky Cemetery,* near the church of the Smolensk Icon of the Mother of God, which is often depicted behind her in icons. Here, where her holy relics[▲]

[+] By the Russian Church Outside Russia (ROCOR), and later by the Moscow Patriarchate in 1988.

[▲] The bones of a saint, which miraculously are preserved after death, lay, thousands visit every year. One can see lines of dozens every day, swelling to hundreds on feast days, lining up to venerate her tomb, light a candle and say a prayer. She is often prayed to for help in finding a job, a home, or a spouse, all of which she renounced in her life.

Churches throughout the world are dedicated to Saint Xenia, and in parishes everywhere, services are sung to her on January 24th (Old Caldendar February 6), her feast day. Countless Orthodox women through the centuries have had Xenia as their patron saint, and icons of her adorn parishes and homes in every country of the world, one would imagine.

Through her extraordinary devotion, the youthful widow exchanged perishable earthly riches and empty pleasures for the imperishable glories of divine love. Humble and humiliated though she was throughout her life, God made her light to shine as from the hilltop, touching countless lives through her example, her prayers, and her miracles.

Holy Saint Xenia, pray to God for us!

---

not succumbing to the natural decomposition one expects. The relics of the saints are often fragrant and some exude oil, called myrrh.

Hymnography for Saint Xenia of St. Petersburg
Feast Day: January 24

TROPARION
Tone 4

Having renounced the vanity of the earthly world,
Thou didst take up the cross of a homeless life of
*   wandering;*
Thou didst not fear grief, privation, nor the mockery of
*   men,*
And didst know the love of Christ.
Now taking sweet delight of this love in heaven,
O Xenia, the blessed and divinely wise,
Pray for the salvation of our souls.

KONTAKION
Tone 3

Having been as a wandering stranger on earth,
sighing for the heavenly homeland,
thou wast known as a fool by the senseless and unbelieving,
but as most wise and holy by the faithful,
and wast crowned by God with glory and honor,
O Xenia, courageous and divinely wise.
Therefore, we cry to thee: Rejoice!
For after earthly wandering thou hast come to dwell in the
*   Father's house.*

EDITORIAL NOTES

This story was originally conceived of,
researched and written by Zenovia Kotsonis,
who began the work at age 72, without having
previously written anything professionally,
because of her devotion to Saint Xenia.
Author Cheryl Tuggle (*Unexpeted Joy*,
Anaphora Press, 2011) graciously worked on
the chapters set in Leningrad. Jeannette's
daughter, Aliki Los and Macrina Lewis, editor,
polished the chapters on Saint Xenia. Many
hands were blessed to bring Ms. Kotsonis'
original vision to fruition, through the prayers
of our Blessed Xenia, whom we all looked to
throughout this work as our teacher and
guide.

Although this story contains hagiographical
elements, it is fictionalized. We can only guess
at the thoughts, words, and feelings of this
saint of God who transcended the bounds of
this world and entered a sphere of life far
removed from our temporal existence and the
cares of this world we carry so heavily. This is
why much of our imaginative story-telling for
her, though informed by historical research
and firm footing within Orthodox tradition in
our own lives, takes place in Xenia's earlier
years, before she had progressed to sanctity.
The details of her later sainthood have been
taken from reputable Orthodox sources.

Two Tales of One City